Spy Night on Union Station

EarthCent Ambassador Series:

Date Night on Union Station

Alien Night on Union Station

High Priest on Union Station

Spy Night on Union Station

Carnival on Union Station

Wanderers on Union Station

Vacation on Union Station

Guest Night on Union Station

Word Night on Union Station

Party Night on Union Station

Book Four of EarthCent Ambassador

Spy Night on Union Station

One

"In conclusion, it is the view of Union Station Embassy that our lack of timely intelligence puts us at a severe disadvantage in all negotiations and interactions with the other species, and although we aren't aware of any imminent threats to Earth or the human Diaspora, that may just be because we aren't looking in the right places. Uh, actually, the preceding view is Ambassador McAllister's, but she's out on maternity leave. It's a boy, by the way, and she said to point out that you'd know that already if you had an intelligence service, though I'm sure she doesn't mean that you should start spying on EarthCent employees. She just meant it as a joke, and maybe she didn't want me to repeat—oh drat. Libby? Can I start over?"

"Of course, Aisha," the station librarian replied. "The report isn't a live feed so you have to say 'send' before I release it to EarthCent. And it's late Friday night at EarthCent headquarters, so there's no hurry."

"Thanks, Libby. I don't know why I'm so nervous. I already did this report once before when the ambassador was on Kasil. Maybe it's because Kelly said she's taking the full six months, and instead of being just an intern, I'm now the temporary acting junior consul. Just to make sure I understand, will the report go out if I say 'send' in

1

context, like, 'The Embassy requests you send help' or something like that?"

"The office doesn't have its own dedicated communications equipment, so you're really talking to me the whole time," Libby explained patiently. "The Stryx give EarthCent a free pass for handling the basic office infrastructure, which really means the local station librarian gets stuck doing all of the work. So don't worry about sending the report before you have a version that will make Kelly proud."

"That could take a while," Aisha said dismally. "And the truth is, I don't understand why the ambassador is worried about us not having an intelligence service. Don't we already get more news than we can keep up with from all the human traders and crews who come through the station? Joe says, if you aren't too particular about your company and you're willing to spend a few creds on drinks, you can find out what's going on anywhere in the galaxy without ever leaving the station, just by hanging out in bars."

"If you've started spending your nights in bars since your marriage, I'll give up on human matchmaking," Libby replied.

"That's not what I was trying to say," Aisha amended herself hastily. "I meant that I don't see the need for professional spies if anybody can gather intelligence from bars here on the station."

"Who would you suggest sending?" Libby prodded the girl gently.

Aisha leaned back from the display desk and stared at the ceiling, a habit she had picked up from Kelly, and tried to think a move ahead. She was well aware by this point that Libby, and the Stryx in general, preferred the Socratic method over simply answering the questions asked by humans. It helped to explain why the children attending the Stryx school always struck visitors as so precocious. Paul encouraged her to think of these conversations with the Stryx like a game of chess. So rather than replying immediately, she considered what Libby might say in response to a number of answers and skipped to the conclusion.

"You're saying that whether it's sitting in a bar and listening to tipsy traders or reading the news in thousands of different languages, somebody has to be responsible for gathering and analyzing information?" Aisha summarized tentatively. "But if we start spying on the other species, won't that make them suspicious that we're planning something?"

"Do the other species spy on humans?" Libby parried Aisha's question.

"I guess Kelly told me that some of the other ambassadors as good as admitted they were spying on EarthCent the first time she met them," Aisha confessed. "But that doesn't mean they expect us to spy back on them."

"When you stop on the Shuk deck to buy vegetables for cooking, do you expect the vendors to charge you, or to offer them as gifts?" Libby asked.

"To charge me, of course," Aisha answered immediately, before remembering her husband's advice to look a move ahead. "I mean, yes, of course I expect them to charge me because that's normal, and if they didn't take my money, I'd be suspicious that they wanted something else in return. Are you saying that the other species are suspicious of us because we don't spy on them?"

"I'm saying that most of the other species see you as being overly dependent on us," Libby chided the young temporary acting junior consul.

"But the Stryx must know more about what's going on in the galaxy than all of the alien intelligence services put together. Wouldn't you just tell us if there was something we needed to know about? Or maybe we could pay you?" she added slyly.

"You know better than that, Aisha," the station librarian admonished the young diplomat as if she were a lazy student. "We've been able to keep the peace in our area of influence for millions of years because we are seen as both neutral and largely benevolent. While many of the advanced species grumble about living in a 'nanny galaxy,' few of them are actually interested in the alternative of competing power-blocs, which inevitably leads to war. So they rely on our tunnel network for trade, and on our Stryx cred register network, which is responsible for the vast majority of inter-species financial transactions where barter isn't an option. But if they came to believe that we were spying on them for the sake of humanity, Pax Stryxa would unravel in short order."

"So, no, wait a minute," Aisha cut herself off from answering too quickly once again. She hadn't played chess in her youth, and she often complained to Paul that she would be progressing faster in their games if he would just let her win once in a while, but he insisted that she wouldn't learn anything if he played poorly on purpose. Lately, she had taken to waiting until he drank a couple of beers with Joe before suggesting a game, but it hadn't helped.

What was it Kelly had said about intelligence? Aisha was so against the idea of spying from the moment the

4

ambassador mentioned it that she hadn't paid close attention to the older woman's reasoning. There was something about the need to build up a network of reliable sources and handlers over a long period of time, and something else about the fact that the other species traded intelligence with each other.

"Kelly said that EarthCent lacks the institutional knowledge to create an intelligence agency and that it would be hard to get started with nothing to build on," Aisha said. "She even suggested that we might get help from the Drazens, though she doesn't want to approach Ambassador Bork about it without checking with EarthCent first."

"Knock, knock," Libby announced. "You have a visitor arriving in five, four, three, two, one…"

"Hey, best friend-in-law," Blythe announced herself cheerily. She strode into the ambassador's office like she owned the embassy, which wasn't that far from the truth. In a late night brainstorming session with her mother and Kelly over the chronically low funding levels at EarthCent, Blythe had come up with the "Adopt an Embassy" campaign. To help launch the project, BlyChas offered to match the contributions to EarthCent embassies on all of the Stryx stations where InstaSitter operated. Six months later, the girls were contributing more to the admittedly small operating budgets of the EarthCent embassies than the Stryx.

"Blythe! I didn't know you were back from your honeymoon," Aisha replied happily. Her guilt feelings over stealing Paul from his former girlfriend were greatly assuaged when Blythe and Clive had tied the knot the previous month.

"I just came from visiting Kelly and the baby," Blythe reported. "She asked me drop in and give you a pep talk about spying because you seemed uncomfortable with the subject."

"Of course I'm uncomfortable with spying," Aisha exclaimed. "Don't you agree that the only way to establish trust is by trusting?"

"Wow, you really are naïve," Blythe said sympathetically. She helped herself to the chair next to Kelly's display desk. "Everybody spies on everybody else, except for EarthCent, that is, which is why so few of the aliens trust us. They think we're up to something."

"How do you know that?" Aisha demanded with more force than she was usually able to muster when talking with Blythe.

"They tell me," Blythe replied bluntly. "It used to only come up once in a while, but since InstaSitter started running ads with the 'Proud Sponsor of EarthCent' tagline, the alien entrepreneurs I meet on the stations assume that BlyChas has taken over the human government. So they pepper me with questions about secret treaties, since they're positive we must be getting intelligence from somewhere. If EarthCent doesn't establish a spy network soon, nobody is going to want to be friends with us. In fact, the Dollnick we had managing InstaSitter on Hearth Station actually tried to sell me some secrets, in the theory that InstaSitter is really a cover operation for the human intelligence service."

"Did you pass them on to Kelly?" Aisha asked.

"Of course not," Blythe replied. "It was a misinformation campaign. I had to fire the manager because I didn't want a Dollnick double agent supervising babysitters."

"But how did you know that the secrets were fakes and that the Dollnick was a double agent?" Aisha asked.

"Are you serious?" Blythe questioned her friend in return. "If the Dollnick wasn't a double agent, he wouldn't be offering to spy for us. The Dollys may be a little rough around the edges, but they aren't traitors."

"I hate this part of diplomacy," Aisha declared. "Why can't we all just be truthful and cooperate?"

"It sounds to me like you're confusing diplomacy with being a librarian," Blythe observed. "My mom told me long ago that the only oath EarthCent insisted employees swear is that they do their best for humanity. If a bunch of aliens came around asking you how to get a special import license for Earth, and what sorts of bacteria are best for killing humans, do you think it's your job to supply the information? EarthCent wants to encourage commerce with the other species, but only where humans get something positive in return. You have to look at diplomatic issues through a filter of what's good for humans first, and how that affects our relations with other species second. Aren't I right, Libby?"

"I might have chosen a profession other than librarian for your example, but on the whole, it's a fair description for a diplomatic service," the Stryx librarian replied testily. "And I would point out to Aisha that without timely intelligence, it's hard to know whether an offer is good or bad."

"But it's spying!" Aisha wailed comically. "It's practically synonymous with cheating and lying. Haven't you ever heard that cheaters never prosper?"

"You're sort of changing the subject, but I have to say that in my experience, cheaters do pretty well," Blythe answered. "Did you ever hear that one, Libby?"

"I've heard it, but only from humans," Libby replied. "Among the species who currently maintain a diplomatic presence on Union Station, it's far more common for parents to tell their children that an honest man can't be cheated."

"That doesn't even make sense!" Aisha protested. "I would have said that you can only cheat honest people. If somebody is dishonest, then cheating them is just trying to break even. Oh, now you're getting me confused."

"Try to think of it as a diplomatic forecast rather than spying," Blythe offered helpfully. "I've never been to Earth myself, but I know from the immersives that most planets have this weather thing, where you can be walking along outside, and then all of a sudden, you can drown or freeze to death. Everybody pays for weather intelligence so they can be prepared."

"It's not that bad," Aisha said in defense of nature, reflecting at the same time that even Blythe didn't know everything. "I mean, some people drown in monsoons every year or get killed by mudslides or tsunamis, but the weather forecasts aren't always that reliable. Come to think of it, I guess we did spend a lot of time talking about the weather on Earth."

"You see?" Blythe said triumphantly. "And did your neighbors think you were spying on them if you peeked over the wall to see if they had a tsunami on their property?"

"But there's still a difference," Aisha argued, letting the other girl's confusion over weather events pass without comment. She recognized in herself the familiar feeling of beginning to give in to Blythe's point of view. "If you wanted to invest in systems to protect humans from asteroids and comets or to predict when a star might go nova, I'd support you one hundred percent. But Kelly was talking about trying to find out ahead of time which aliens are building new orbitals or factory-farms, where they are exploring for new worlds, what secret treaties they're signing with each other. That's not the same as the weather."

"Sure it is," Blythe insisted. "It's like a force of nature that's outside of our control, but we still have to be ready to deal with it when it comes. What happens to all of the human farmers and sharecroppers if an advanced species starts a mechanized orbital factory-farm producing human food at a fraction of the cost? Wouldn't you want us to know about that before the market is flooded? And do you want generation after generation of humans to grow up on colony ships without ever finding a home, because everywhere they choose to explore has already been taken? And why shouldn't EarthCent know which aliens are secretly cooperating to advance their business interests at our expense? When it comes down to it, all espionage is industrial espionage."

"Is it really that bad, Libby?" Aisha asked.

"You have to look out for yourself in this galaxy," the Stryx admitted. "Ignorance is never a defense. And if you know what's coming and you have good leadership, you can settle most problems before they turn serious."

"Alright, I think I'm ready now," Aisha conceded with a sigh. "If I just dictate a new conclusion, can you add it to the routine stuff?"

"Of course," Libby replied. "Here, let me play back your last thought and then you can continue."

The two young women listened as Aisha's disembodied voice, which somehow sounded more mature and professional than the real thing, filled the room.

"On Wednesday, I met with the Sharf Emissary to Union Station, where we learned to our mutual dissatisfaction that humans are allergic to Sharf skin-and-scale polish. The Sharf is visiting the station as part of a delegation from the unaligned industrial empires, a group I could find no mention of in the EarthCent diplomatic organizations directory, despite the popularity of used Sharf vessels among wealthy humans. Before my face puffed up to the point that I could barely see and had to leave the reception, I heard a disturbing rumor about another off-network species, the Mengoth, who supposedly have it in for humans because we remind them of a race they once served as slaves."

"Cue, Aisha," Libby interjected.

"In conclusion, it is the view of Union Station Embassy that a lack of intelligence forecasts puts us at a severe disadvantage in all negotiations and interactions with other species. In some cases, our absence on the espionage front may actually be making the aliens nervous, so we encourage EarthCent to begin the work of building an intelligence agency as soon as possible. On a personal note, Ambassador McAllister gave birth to a baby boy on Monday, and she joked that if EarthCent had an intelligence service, she might have received some flowers."

Two

The galactic EarthCent Intelligence building in New York City came as a complete disappointment to Lynx Edgehouse, who was at least expecting a doorman. Instead, she found herself struggling to read the white plastic letters of an ancient building directory behind a dull pane of glass that might have gone years without cleaning. After a quick look around to make sure she was unobserved, she spit on the glass and then tried to clean a spot with the sleeve of the ratty winter overcoat she'd just bought for one cred at a thrift shop.

Acme Exporters – B201

B as in basement? She squinted in the dim light of the lobby, scanning the rest of the directory for another Acme suite, but B201 was it. She double-checked the scrap of paper that the contact man had slipped into her pocket after they exchanged the pre-arranged sign at the spaceport diner, but her memory was unfortunately correct.

What would my father do if he was standing here in my shoes, Lynx asked herself. The answer came to her immediately, and she fished in her belt pouch for a coin. Apparently, she had used up all of her small change in tips or at the peanut dispenser in the bar, because all that she had left was the programmable cred from her Stryx mini-register. The coin's passive display was flat on both sides so it always flipped true, one side displaying her embarrassingly low account balance, the other side an image of one of the Stryx stations that anchored the galaxy's transportation network.

"Creds, I keep going, station, I go home," she declared, flipping the coin in the air. Although the coins were reputed to be nearly indestructible, she made the mid-air catch and slapped it on the back of her hand rather than letting it bounce off the floor. "Creds."

Feeling depressed and trapped at the same time, Lynx punched the down button to summon an elevator. After a long minute, the metal doors to her left slid open, though not quite all the way, increasing her trepidation. Entering the elevator, she ran her finger down the matrix of old-fashioned buttons until she reached B at the bottom left corner. Just B? No B2? She let out a defeated sigh and pressed the button.

The complaining whirr of machinery was accompanied by a sudden jerk and a loud clank, leading Lynx to flex her knees in anticipation of a hard landing. Instead, after a horrible grating sound followed by the lights going out and then blinking back on, the elevator staggered to a halt. The metal door twitched several times, after which the first section slid partway open and stopped. The elevator car had halted well short of the floor, and the door wouldn't budge when she pushed on it, nor would it respond to the button.

Suddenly it struck her that this was all a test and she smiled grimly. If EarthCent Intelligence wanted their agent recruits to prove their unflappability, she was just the girl for the job. Removing her bulky cloth coat, she tossed it through the opening to the basement floor, and with one fluid movement she slipped down after it, landing on her feet. A man with immersive-star looks rose from the old wooden chair next to the only door in sight, clapping slowly in appreciation of her performance.

"You must be Lynx," he pronounced in a burred accent she couldn't quite place. "They call me A.P. Malloy. The Old Man is waiting for you inside."

"Did I pass the elevator test?" Lynx inquired archly.

"The elevator is broken," he replied with an infuriating superiority that gave the impression of coming from old wealth, private schools, fast cars and long days at the polo grounds. But then he bent to retrieve her coat, brushing it off at the risk of getting dust on his own immaculate suit, and hung it on a bright red valve that was either a control for an ancient steam heating circuit or a shut-off for a sprinkler system. "The building has been condemned for some time, but the Old Man insists it's perfect for our purposes and that taking the stairs is good for physical conditioning. Just knock and walk right in."

The frosted glass of the door was carefully lettered 'Acme Exporters', with 'B201' centered just below, so Lynx tapped the door frame twice with her knuckles, turned the old brass knob, and entered.

"Please take a seat and I'll be with you in a minute." The man behind the sole desk in the narrow room spoke without raising his head. Other than the single wooden chair whose mate was currently in the hall outside the door, the space was uncluttered by furnishings or equipment of any sort. Lynx seated herself and took advantage of the time to study the person whom she hoped to soon be calling the "Old Man" herself.

As a description, the nom-de-guerre was entirely accurate, since the man looked to be well past his prime and accelerating towards decrepitude. His appearance reminded her of a common plot element in the old spy movies she had watched on long jumps, the retired war horse called back to action to clean up an intelligence service after it was penetrated by the enemy.

Other than a massive, old-fashioned watch on his right wrist, he wore no jewelry. Right wrist makes him a southpaw, Lynx noted to herself. He sported thick eyeglasses with heavy black plastic frames, giving him an anachronistic look in a world where even the poorest of the poor could afford walk-in robotic laser surgery at train station kiosks to correct most vision problems. An affectation? A disguise? His suit looked like nothing Lynx had ever come across in her wide travels, but maybe it was the current style for the upper crust of Earth society. She had only been to Earth a half a dozen times, and aside from a bit of tourism on the first trip, she hadn't stayed around any longer than business required.

"I'm Director Fordham," he finally introduced himself, setting aside the file in which Lynx knew her entire life would be laid bare, down to the most personal details. She couldn't even imagine the resources EarthCent Intelligence could call on, and she only hoped that a few of the less fortunate incidents she'd been tangled up in while trading far off the Stryx tunnel network had escaped their notice. "You are Lynx Hedgehouse?"

"Edgehouse," she corrected him.

The Director scowled, and taking up the file again, scribbled on the sheets of paper in several different places. Lynx didn't know if he was making notes to fire various clerks for incompetence, or simply scratching out the capital 'H' wherever her name appeared.

"Can't afford display tabs?" she joked, hoping to steer the conversation onto a friendly path.

Fordham's head jerked up in surprise and his features quickly resolved themselves into a frown. Lynx shifted uneasily in her chair when he didn't speak immediately, kicking herself for trying to make a joke so early in the interview. It wouldn't be the first time her sense of humor had gotten her into trouble.

"Paper is the safest technology for keeping secrets," he said finally. "All other forms of recordkeeping and communications can be hacked, altered or intercepted by aliens with superior technology. And if you're in a tough spot, you can always eat the paper. Try doing that with a display tab."

"Got it, sir," Lynx responded with alacrity. "Should I use pen or pencil?"

Fordham fixed her with an intense stare and paused again, as if trying to decide whether she was making fun of him. Realizing too late that her quick response might have labeled her a wisecracker, Lynx waited on tenterhooks for his response.

"Pen," he declared after a long wait. "Unless you can't find one, in which case pencil will suffice."

The Director and the potential agent regarded one another in silence for another long moment, and Lynx began to wonder if she had already failed the interview and he was simply waiting for her to figure it out for herself.

"Right, then," Fordham suddenly declared. "You'll be partnered with A.P. Malloy, our best agent. Do you have any questions before I call him in?"

Lynx was so taken aback by the news that she had passed the interview and was about to become an EarthCent Intelligence agent that she was almost speechless. Almost. But her lifelong habit of asking questions that nobody wanted to hear overcame her initial shock, and she rapidly organized her thoughts into a prioritized list of points that needed clarification.

"I do have just a few questions," Lynx admitted, holding up her hand with her thumb and forefinger spread about an inch apart to indicate that she would only take a little of his valuable time. "I never actually heard of EarthCent Intelligence before I was, er, recruited at the Space Rats bar last night, and I don't really remember too much of the conversation. In fact, I wasn't sure if it really happened until your messenger did the nose-rub signal and slipped the address in my pocket at the spaceport diner this morning."

The Director merely lifted one bushy grey eyebrow at this story and waited for her to continue.

"So, and I don't want you to take this the wrong way because I really want to serve humanity and I think I'll be a great secret agent, but I can't help wondering how I was chosen. I spotted your recruiter at least an hour before he approached me. I thought he was just another jerk hitting on all the single women at the bar. But he explained right off that it was just a cover and he was there specifically to meet me."

"Are you familiar with the recruitment process for the EarthCent Diplomatic corps?" the Director asked without his usual pause, as if he expected her question and was prepared with an answer.

"Of course," she replied. "I always hoped I would hear from them out of the blue, but by the time I was twenty-four, I knew it wasn't going to happen. I guess it didn't occur to me that EarthCent Intelligence would work the same way."

"If that's it, I'll call in A.P. Malloy now," the Director said, reaching for the button on the front of his desk that looked like a salvaged doorbell. The wires ran to the edge of the desk that abutted the wall, where they hung down from a steam pipe, around which they were wrapped in a slow spiral like a growing vine. The pipe disappeared through the front wall to the right of the door, and if Lynx was correct, the wires must have come out in the hall just around the improvised coat rack.

"Hold on just a second," Lynx pleaded, leaning forward and seizing Fordham's hand before he could press the button. The Director froze like a statue, then he slowly relaxed and settled ponderously back into his chair.

"As you wish," he replied after a long pause, during which she wasn't sure if he was staring at her or through her.

"It's just that I'm very curious," Lynx said apologetically. "That's part of why I think I'll be a natural at intelligence work. I just can't help wondering how EarthCent finally spotted me after I gave up, even though it's intelligence work rather than diplomacy. I'm twenty-eight now, you know, and I've spent most of the last ten years trading around the fringes of Stryx space. Were you keeping tabs on me the whole time?"

The Director drummed his fingers on the table for a moment and appeared to be listening intently to the rhythmic sound produced. Then he smiled for the first time and gave the exact response she wanted to hear.

"I think you've answered your own question," Fordham told her. "And there's no better cover story for an agent than that of the independent trader. You can go anywhere at any time, and as long as you make a profit, nobody will question your motives."

Lynx found herself relaxing a little, since nothing put her at ease more than being told she was right.

"I guess I was afraid that your recruiter was just asking women at random," she confessed with a laugh. "Well, not exactly random, as I did notice he only approached women with red hair."

"EarthCent has had very good luck with redheads," the director replied, before harpooning her with his intense stare. "You don't dye your hair, do you?"

"Not me," she replied earnestly, though the question chipped into the pleasure she had experienced over being chosen for her unique talents as a trader and fearless adventurer. Maybe this was one instance where the less she knew the better, and she decided to stop asking questions lest she discover her main qualification for intelligence work was her shoe size. But she still had to ask about training. "Will the training program take a long time? I have to know whether to leave my ship docked at the elevator anchor, or to move it into a parking orbit."

"Docked at the elevator anchor is perfect," the Director replied after his characteristic pause. "Our training program is based on an apprenticeship in the field. There are also some training materials you'll need to study in your free time, of course. Now, if that's everything?" He reached cautiously for the doorbell, and getting no reaction from Lynx, pressed the button. When nothing happened, no chimes or buzzes, Fordham stabbed the button again, several times. For a moment he looked like he was ready to tear the device from the desk and throw it at the door, but he quickly regained control over his emotions and nodded to Lynx, saying, "Could you?"

Lynx rose from her chair and went to open the door and summon her soon-to-be partner, but the brass handle came away in her hand as the other end fell into the hallway with a clatter. She realized that there was a square shaft sticking out of the heavy handle she still held, so she fit it through the hole in the lock plate and turned. The door pushed open from the outside.

"I'll fix that," Malloy said, holding the door halfway open. "The set screw backed out, see? We'll just put the handle back on the shaft and tighten the screw. It'll be good for another hundred years." Then he pulled an elaborate Swiss Army knife from his pocket and pried out the screwdriver attachment with a well-manicured thumbnail. In less than a minute, the repair was complete, and Lynx found herself standing side-by-side with Mr. Fixit in front of the Director's desk. She had the weird feeling that Fordham was a justice of the peace and the two agents were getting married.

"I'm sure I don't have to explain to the two of you the responsibilities and the sacred nature of a partnership between agents," the Director spoke solemnly, giving Lynx the impression that he was reading from a prepared speech. "You will be living together in close quarters for long periods of time, so it's of the utmost importance that you also respect each other's privacy and remember that you are professionals doing a job, not just casual shipmates."

"Shipmates?" Lynx asked in surprise. "It never occurred to me that I'd have to give up my ship to join, though I guess it makes sense you'd have some super-fast spy ship loaded with advanced weaponry for agents."

"Quite the contrary," the Director reassured her. "A secret agent's only meaningful defense is a solid cover story. You and your ship are known quantities on the fringes of Stryx space, and you are to avoid confrontations at all costs."

"So we'll both be traveling in my ship?" Lynx asked, squinting at the Director through one eye, her default facial expression when striking a bargain for a cargo. Despite her relief that she could take the job without putting her ship into cold storage, she was beginning to feel a twinge of trader's doubt as to the pocketbook of her new employers. "I don't want to sound like a mercenary, but will there be any compensation?"

"EarthCent Intelligence agents can expect to earn as much as ambassadors," he told her sternly. "Your salaries and ship expenses will be paid out of your trading profits, the remainder of which you will remit to the home office."

"So, I'll be working as a trader, just like I've done for the last ten years, except now, I'll be paying salaries to Agent Malloy and myself, and anything left over goes to you?" she recapped slowly, hoping that there was an error of logic in her formulation.

"Exactly," Fordham confirmed her suspicion. "Of course, we will provide a suitable starting cargo. We understand that you've had certain difficulties in the last year and have been seeking consignment goods."

Lynx flinched at the Director's words, which were unfortunately true. If he had said, "reduced to seeking consignment goods," the description would have been even more accurate. Nine years of careful trading had allowed her to pay off the mortgage on her ship ahead of schedule, but something had changed the instant she didn't have a regular payment to make. She had started taking stupid risks in search of a big score, even flying empty in preference to taking subsistence cargoes, and the last year had eaten through her savings. Her tunnel transit to Earth was only made possible by the charitable policy that the Stryx maintained towards human traders.

"And our mission?" Lynx inquired, striving to formulate the question in as few words as possible.

The Director pushed back his chair and slid open the wide, shallow desk drawer, removing a dingy white envelope that looked like something from the twenty century. He looked at the envelope, looked at the agents, shook his head, and then extended it towards them. Lynx and A.P. both grabbed for it, but Lynx was the faster of the two. She had never held a paper envelope in her hands before. It appeared to be glued shut in some way, and she was unsure how to proceed.

"Not here," the Director said. "Open it when you get back to your ship. Your cargo is already waiting at the anchor satellite where you docked. Welcome to EarthCent Intelligence. And remember, if you're caught, there will be no help from Earth. We'll deny any knowledge of your existence."

"Thank you," Lynx said, even though she wondered what she was thanking him for. Then she stiffened as a hand pressed against her side, but it was just her new partner guiding her to the door. The handle worked perfectly, as A.P. had promised. He led her past the stalled elevator to another door, where they found the emergency stairs to the main lobby and exited the condemned building.

Three

"Welcome to the first meeting of the EarthCent Intelligence Committee, and let me thank those of you on different time schedules who woke up in the middle of the night to join the holoconference call. I want you all to know that while I can see you and you can see me, the hologram you see of the other committee members is being run through an anonymity filter. I point this out so you don't mistakenly believe that all of your colleagues have escaped from a wildlife sanctuary. Also, our research department reports that it is traditional for members of secret committees to use code names, and I've chosen 'Home Boy' for myself. Are there any questions before we begin?"

"How do you pronounce the acronym?"

"Could you be a little more specific?" Home Boy inquired in response. "And please, everybody, give a code name before you speak so we'll know who is who."

"Uh, Belinda," the woman replied. "I don't want to have to say 'EarthCent Intelligence Committee' every time I refer to our group. But I'm not sure how to pronounce ECIC. E-KICK?"

"Troll here. I vote for ignoring the capital 'C' in 'EarthCent' and going with EIC. Then we could pronounce it as ICE."

"Toto here. How did you get from EIC to ICE? If anything, I'd pronounce EIC as EEK! And I thought there was an ambassador named Belinda on..."

"No names," Home Boy cut Toto off mid-sentence. "Belinda, please choose a different code name, one that doesn't incorporate any elements from your personal name. Troll, I have to agree that EEK makes more sense, but we may as well put it to a vote since that's what committees do. All in favor of ICE, raise a hand. That's one, two. Now all in favor of EEK raise a hand. That's one, two, three. So the vote is three-to-two in favor of EEK with two abstentions."

"Who abstains from voting on an acronym?" Toto asked in frustration.

"Pill Bottle here. I abstained," said a man in an immaculate five-piece suit, the only attendee who had dressed formally for the holoconference. The anonymity filter had replaced his head with that of a baby elephant, which looked quite sophisticated in the suit, especially while elevating its trunk and mouthing the English words in perfect synchronization with the speaker.

"Lion here. I abstained as well," admitted a sleepy-looking chimp wearing either a silk kimono or pajamas.

"Cowardly," Toto muttered under her breath, but loudly enough for everybody to hear.

There was an awkward pause before Home Boy cleared his throat and asked, "Did everybody have a chance to watch the interview video? Just say 'No' if you didn't have the opportunity yet. Everybody watched it? Great. My team here feels that the actor we chose to play the director did an excellent job, although he did rely heavily on subvocing for help whenever an unexpected question came up."

"Don't you think calling the actor playing the head of the agency a director is confusing?" asked the woman formerly known as Belinda, whose head had been swapped with that of a giant talking carp.

"Calling it an agency definitely makes it confusing," Troll agreed. "All we need now is a producer and we'll be in the immersive business."

"Could we just let all of that slide for the moment?" Home Boy requested, suddenly sounding very tired. "Does anybody have any constructive feedback about the recruitment process?"

"The office was an embarrassment, and I'm surprised Lynx didn't walk out on us," Toto commented. By chance or design, her code name was a perfect match for the Cairn terrier head that the other committee members saw speaking. "And while I agree that her profile is just what we were looking for, her story about being contacted in a bar didn't give me great confidence in the field recruiter."

"Yes, that was unfortunate," Home Boy replied. "The field agent our office hired to do the recruitment got cold feet at the last minute, so we had to use the director's agent."

"Tinkerbelle here. I thought the director was an actor," objected a python-faced woman wearing what looked like a white nightgown. Her forked tongue darted out to test the air between each word, leading some of the others to suspect that the anonymity filter was just showing off. "Where did he get his own agents?"

"Agent as in booking agent," Home Boy explained. "We found the director through a talent agency, so we asked his agent to provide another actor for the field agent role. Apparently, when he heard that the job included approaching young women visiting Earth, the director's agent chose himself for the assignment. We won't make that mistake again."

"If we agree that he got the right candidate in the end, why not continue to use him?" Troll asked.

"Interesting," Home Boy replied. "Any thoughts?"

"Well, I guess the Stryx would keep him in place," Toto mused. "It's just that he sounds kind of sleazy."

"Spying is a sleazy business," Lion pointed out archly.

"Alright, then. If nobody objects, we'll keep the director and the field recruiter in place, but we'll find a new office space for Acme Exporters," Home Boy summarized.

"I think we're heading for a disaster if we have to explain which kind of director or agent we're talking about every time we have a discussion," the carp pointed out. "I wouldn't want to accidentally send an actor to do an agent's work."

"It's three o'clock in the morning here and you animals are talking in riddles!" the chimp complained, scratching his side through his silk top. "Can't we just forget about the fact that we're relying on people from the entertainment industry to help get the recruiting off the ground? From now on, let's only talk about the real agents and director."

"Second the motion," Lion chipped in.

"Any objections?" Home Boy asked. "No? Great, though I should remind you that we don't have a real director yet, which is why we hired an actor." The animals all grimaced at this last comment, with the chimp looking especially fearsome.

"Do you have any candidates for a real director?" Toto inquired. "I understand we can't rely on the Stryx to do the recruiting as they do for EarthCent, but leaving the job unfilled during the start-up phase doesn't make any sense."

"Are you trying to keep the Stryx in the dark about EarthCent Intelligence?" asked the elephant.

"Not while we're using their tunneling real-time communications network," Troll replied. Nobody's code name was more incongruous than Troll's, whose head had been replaced by that of a bird of paradise.

"Are you saying that the Stryx can break the encryption on the secure channels?" asked the former Belinda.

"Who do you think is doing the encryption and decryption?" Troll pointed out.

"Uh, nobody in this case," Home Boy interjected.

"I knew there was something missing!" Toto exclaimed. "I've been on secure conference calls with aliens, and there's always a little red lock symbol in the upper right corner of the hologram!"

"The first meeting of EEK, and you cheapskates couldn't pay for a secure channel?" Troll asked in disgust.

"It costs three thousand cred for a seven-way, it just wasn't in the budget," Home Boy defended himself. "If I had listened to the bean-counters, the whole meeting would have been voice-only."

"Maybe we should have discussed these issues through paper correspondence," Tinkerbelle suggested. "If there's a security breach, we can always eat the paper."

"Brilliant!" Troll contributed sarcastically.

"Perhaps this is a good time to discuss our budgetary constraints," Home Boy said. "Do any of you have any extra funds in the budget you'd like to remit to EarthCent HQ?"

"No!" the attendees chorused.

"How about something like the 'Adopt an Embassy' campaign?" Toto suggested. "It's really the business community that's pushed the hardest for us to establish an intelligence service, so they might pony up."

"Adopt a spy?" Home Boy said out loud, as if testing the catchiness of the phrase. "I'm not sure."

"Maybe if we did it privately," Troll suggested. "I don't think we want to see any 'Proud sponsor of EarthCent Intelligence' ads from InstaSitter."

"I love their ads," the former Belinda commented. "The little red-headed girl is an angel. I can't believe anybody could charge to babysit for her."

"Me either," Toto replied, suddenly warming to the talking carp head. "Maybe we could kill two birds with one stone and find a director who's willing to fund EarthCent Intelligence? No offence about the bird thing, Troll."

"That's really not a bad idea," Troll mused. "And if we keep hiring agents who own two-man ships and can pay themselves out of their own trading profits, it shouldn't even cost that much. Just rent for an office and some support staff."

"All in favor of Toto finding us a wealthy director, raise your hands," Home Boy declared. "One, two, three, four, five, six. All against? One. Sorry, Toto. You're outvoted six-to-one."

"Alright," Toto barked, realizing she'd been hoisted by her own petard. "I've got one or two people in mind. But they're good, so don't come crying to me if one of them accepts and stages a putsch."

"Who would want to take over EarthCent?" Home Boy asked incredulously. "I've been trying to quit for years but the Stryx keep rejecting my resignation. Would any of you like to come back to Earth and take over?" Everybody waited in silence. "Anyone? Alright then. If we could get back to business, the main item on the agenda is to create a charter for the agency that sets down in black-and-white the scope of intelligence operations. Obviously, we don't expect to get this done today, but if you would suggest your priorities, my staff can put together a working document for the next meeting to critique. Shall we start with Bel—I mean, Mrs. Carp?"

"I'll come up with a new code name for the next meeting," Belinda promised, her fish lips puckering as she spoke. "You just caught me unawares. As to priorities, we need to know about everything that affects humanity. The only intelligence I get these days comes from hanging out in bars and reading digests of alien news broadcasts, which are probably propaganda."

"We're all aware of the lack of intelligence, that's why we're here," Home Boy admonished her. "What I'd like from you now is just your top concerns. This isn't an exclusionary process, you can always add to it later. We just need a starting point to draft an operating charter."

"Well, military capabilities, obviously," she stated. "The Stryx are pretty close-mouthed about the alien fleets because they consider it competitive information. Even though we don't have any warships ourselves, it would be useful to know what our colony ships and traders can expect to run into when they jump away from the tunnel network. And who is competing with us directly for markets and resources, the Stryx are absolutely silent on that point. The local merchants know more about it than I do. Uh, that's just two, right? So I guess it would be useful to know more about the relations between the different species, beyond how they act in public. For example, we know that the Drazens and the Hortens hate each other, but maybe it's all a big act."

"Military, markets and inter-species relations," Home Boy summed up. "Pill Bottle?"

"We need to know who is actively expanding," the elephant head replied. "The aliens we're competing with for new colony worlds are the ones who'll need the closest watching. We aren't a military threat to anybody, so we have to look where our commercial interests collide. That would be colonization, providing cheap labor, low-tech manufacturing and farming. Other than that, we need to learn something about the intelligence services we're up against. I've done a bit of asking around, and I get the impression that most of the other species depend heavily on their expatriates to report anything interesting through diplomatic channels. From there it gets passed on to specialists. I didn't count, but that's all I've got."

"Collision points and counterintelligence," Home Boy recapped. "Lion?"

"Military, collision points, and data mining," the chimp replied. "No point in reinventing the wheel on the first two, but I'm concerned with how little I know about the relevant history of the aliens I deal with every day. The Stryx are helpful if I ask the right questions, but there's such a thing as information overload. When I meet an alien delegation, I'd like to know what they had to say to the last dozen or so Stryx fostered species they met, and whether they kept their word."

"Data mining," Home Boy nodded. "Not very sexy, but important. Don't forget to bring it up when you're scouting for a new director, Toto. For every agent in the field, we can probably use several at home, just mining information from publicly available sources. Any priorities of your own?"

"I think we need to keep a close eye on the Vergallians," Toto replied immediately. "They were getting ready to take us over when the Stryx stepped in and opened Earth, and I don't trust them and their Empire of a Hundred Worlds. And though I know in my heart that the Stryx only want the best for us, I think some of their attempts to protect us are childish. Has anybody ever looked at the official holomap of the galaxy that they supply with their quantum-coupled ship controllers? There are whole areas of the galaxy that are cordoned off due to ravenous space monsters, and if you keep zooming in, they actually show up as giant winged things with pointy teeth. What do they eat, stars? The Stryx are just trying to scare us off, so I think some independent surveying or collaboration with other species on map checking is in order."

"Vergallians and mapping," Home Boy noted. "Tinkerbelle?"

"I think we need to know more about magic and mind control," the python replied, looking particularly evil. "Sure, everybody knows that the Vergallian elites can play tricks with pheromones, but that's not the same as being able to reach into somebody's head and control them directly. For all we know, any one of us could already be compromised. And it's not just telepathy we have to worry about, it's magic. If magic is just processes that we aren't smart enough to understand, so be it, but we still have to be prepared to deal with them."

"Magic and telepathy, very good," Home Boy acknowledged. "And that leaves, Troll?"

"I was going to say mind control," the bird of paradise squawked. "Anyway, somebody else mentioned points of collision, but I think we need to pay more attention to points of exclusion. If all the other species are nuts over something we've never heard of, whether it's a source of food, a game, or a new way of singing Happy Birthday, there's probably a good reason. I think all of the points brought up here are very good, but they're mainly reactive. I think we need to be proactive. After all, the best defense is a good offence."

"Well said, well said," Home Boy repeated rapidly. "You've all given us plenty of meat to chew on until the next meeting. As much as I'd like to discuss these points further, I know a couple of you need to get back to sleep, and we only rented the zoo filter for a half an hour, so our time is almost up."

On six Stryx stations scattered around the galaxy, the holographic projections over the display desks of the ambassadors glitched, and the seven humans found themselves looking at each other without the animal filter.

"I guess we'll know for next time to buy an extra minute for the anonymity fil…" The channel cut out before Home Boy could finish his sentence.

Four

"It's funny how cargo loading has come full circle," Lynx commented, as she worked with A.P. to transfer the contents of the elevator container filled with EarthCent-supplied goods into the hold of her small trader. The Prudence was docked at one of the low rent extension spokes of Elevator One's anchor satellite, and the two agents were working rapidly in the Zero-G of the cargo station's geostationary orbit. The tether continued through the anchor satellite to a counterweight that supported the whole elevator structure from further out in space. "I watched a Grenouthian documentary about ocean shipping just a few months ago, and most species ended up using standardized containers that could ride high above the waterline and be easily transferred to ground transportation."

"The large cargo spaceships still use containers, though there are too many different versions to really call any of them standard," A.P. replied. He stowed the case of mixed liquor bottles in the spot Lynx had indicated. "These magnetic cleats keep slipping when you throw me boxes. Just because the weight is gone doesn't mean the mass disappears as well."

"I've been doing this for ten years," Lynx reminded him. "You just need to relax when you catch crates, don't try to stop them dead. Let your arms act like shock absorbers and redirect some of the momentum to conserve energy. Let's just swap places for now. It will be more efficient if you tell me what's in the boxes and I stow them, since I'm the one who knows where to put things."

Both agents momentarily deactivated their magnetic cleats and pushed off, passing each other mid-air as they switched positions. Lynx executed a slow spin and landed gracefully on the open spot she'd chosen in the hold, while A.P. sailed out the cargo hatch and into the elevator container, grabbing the edge to bring himself to a sudden halt.

"Ouch," agent Malloy complained. "I almost tore my arm off."

"Let's go, time is money," Lynx exhorted her partner. "If we can empty the container and get out of here before 24:00, we'll save a whole day's rental on the docking arm. I left the cargo management tab up there. Just read the labels out loud like I've been doing and the tab will add them to the manifest."

"Canned baked beans, one gross," A.P. read the label off the next box, braced his back against the container, and sailed it towards Lynx at nearly twice the speed she had been throwing him boxes. Lynx corralled the case and guided it to the deck in a single fluid movement, letting the ship absorb the kinetic energy.

"That's the ticket," she called to A.P. "Keep them coming and we'll be out of here in no time."

"Hand-made soap, Anne's Boutique, five hundred pieces," A.P. sang out as he sailed her the next box.

"Wow! I guess the Old Man knows something about trading after all," Lynx said as she stowed the soap. "I was beginning to wonder if this whole operation was just some sort of weird experiment, but I have to admit they put together an interesting cargo for a small trader."

"Watch the mass on this one," A.P. warned, sending a box her way at a fraction of the speed he'd thrown the last two. "Hunting knives, Buck 110, one gross. Two of these boxes would weigh more than you down on Earth."

Lynx clicked her heels together to hit the momentary kill switch on the magnet cleats, launched herself straight up to the ceiling of the hold, executed a flip like a competitive swimmer at the end of a pool, and intercepted the box of knives as it drifted by below her, using her momentum to carry it to the deck. She turned back to her partner and clapped her hands, waiting for the next box. He fumbled around for a moment with his back shielding the box and his hands from Lynx, before straightening up and sending it in her direction.

"Synthetic high-temperature lubricant, ten liters," A.P. called as the case floated gently in her direction. "Box has been opened and the flaps are just folded together, so be careful."

"Not exactly a gold mine here," Lynx grumbled as she stowed the box, quickly securing it in place with the thin magnetic cargo webbing "You can buy this stuff on any orbital factory for a song. The artificial people go through it like crazy."

"Decorative rosewood chopsticks, one thousand count," agent Malloy read off the label of the next box, before launching it in her direction.

"Fantastic!" declared his partner as she guided the large box into the perfect space. "I hope there's another box. These things are worth their weight in gold out on the fringe. Well, silver maybe."

"There are three more boxes," A.P. replied as he shoved the second her way. "You must be very good at Tetris."

"What's Tetris?" Lynx asked, as she reoriented the oblong box to fill a matching vacancy.

"It's a computer game," her partner explained. "It involves fitting falling shapes into places at an ever increasing speed."

"Yuck," she replied, fielding the third box. "It does sound like the sort of game computers would play, but why would I be interested?"

"Never mind," A.P. muttered, before sending the fourth box of chopsticks in her direction. He continued to work his way through the loosely packed container. "Ping pong balls? What are we supposed to do with these?"

Lynx caught the large box, read the label herself and shook her head. "If we didn't need to return the container empty, I'd set them aside to leave behind. Well, there's always room in interstellar space."

"Canned dog food, meat-flavored," agent Malloy reported as he sent another box in Lynx's direction.

"Special food for dogs?" Lynx asked in wonder, guiding the incoming projectile to its resting place. "What's the point of that? And what do they mean by meat-flavored? Is it meat or isn't it? Earth is a weird place."

"Winter coats," A.P. read off the next carton. "There's a bunch of these that are taped up with handwritten labels."

"Can't think too much about it now," Lynx replied, stowing the box away and awaiting the next. "We've got to empty the container and get out of here one way or another."

"Paint and chemicals," her partner read off the next box, peeling back the folded-over flaps to look inside.

"This stuff isn't even new. It's like somebody emptied out their garage."

From that point on, the cargo varied between high value items that carried a trade premium, and boxes that looked like they'd been misdirected from somebody who was moving house. Still, the agents finished emptying the container with more than an hour to spare, and A.P. used the long vacuum hose attachment Lynx provided to remove the inevitable dust and bits of small debris from the metal box. Part of the contract for elevator usage specified that containers be returned "broom clean," and in Zero-G, this meant vacuuming them out. Not doing so could result in a cleaning fee, a luxury Lynx couldn't afford.

"We're cleared for departure," the captain of the Prudence reported to her partner, after he returned from hooking the empty container to the wire conveyer drag and joined her on the bridge. Lynx's ship was a standard two-man trader, the generic type used by up-and-coming humanoids who weren't yet manufacturing their own ships and had to make do with little more than customized bathroom attachments for waste disposal. Most cultures shared an apocryphal story about a cheap trader who tried to get by with an alien lavatory, a tale which had grown in length and improbability through countless retellings over intoxicating beverages. Though Lynx didn't consider herself the squeamish type, she was less than comfortable with the idea of sharing the only facilities with a strange man, and hoped they could at least avoid talking about it.

"Have you opened our orders yet?" A.P. inquired.

"I was waiting for you," she confessed, fishing inside of her coveralls for the envelope. "But maybe we should detach from the docking spoke first. I know it's not a Stryx station, but you never know who might be listening in when you're sharing some systems."

"Operational security," her partner acknowledged with a nod. "Good call."

Hah! Passed another test, Lynx said to herself as she initiated the departure sequence. As soon as the docking clamps released, the anchor satellite's manipulator fields took over, guiding the ship through the moderate trading traffic around the elevator and accelerating them on a vector towards the Stryx tunnel, the direction taken by the vast majority of ships.

Both of Earth's orbital elevators had been constructed by a consortium of alien contractors at the request of EarthCent, the loan financing provided by the Stryx, in a successful attempt to help the faltering economy of the planet achieve an acceptable balance of trade. The technology and materials involved in elevator construction were hundreds, if not thousands of years ahead of anything the humans could have managed for themselves. The anchor satellites were operated by young artificial intelligences, usually short-timers who were repaying body mortgages to the Stryx administration for newly recognized AI.

"That's it, then," Lynx said. She relaxed in her command chair as the anchor satellite's manipulator fields released them to coast towards the Stryx tunnel terminal. "We've got a half-an-hour to figure out where we're going before we get to the tunnel. No point in wasting fuel to get there a few minutes quicker."

"What do you think the Old Man has planned for us?" A.P. asked.

Lynx groaned to herself. This business of being an apprentice could turn into a real drag if her partner was going to make every decision into a pop-quiz. Lynx examined the envelope from both sides, trying to figure out the trick to opening it. There seemed to be a sort of triangular flap on the back, but it was glued down so smoothly that she could barely feel the edge with a fingernail.

"I've been thinking about our meeting with the, uh, Old Man," Lynx ventured after a long silence, during which she gave up on getting the envelope opened without using violence. "I know he didn't say anything when he handed over our orders, but you being senior and all, I guess he really intended you to take them." Without releasing her safety harness, she turned to the right and extended the envelope to agent Malloy. "Here, you open them."

A.P. nodded gravely and reached across the central console to take the envelope from Lynx. He studied it for a couple of seconds and then ripped it in two, returning the larger half to his partner. Both eventually figured out how to pop open the walls of the envelope and extract the torn sheet of paper from within.

"Well, this is a dumb technology," Lynx commented, studying her half of the message. "What's the point of a package that forces you to destroy the contents to get it open?"

"Beats me," A.P. responded. "My half says, '*Your training mission is*, uh, next line, *penetrate Farling home system*, next line, *destroy this message*.'"

"My half says, '*Top secret*, next line, *to acquire Farling mind control drugs. Do not*, next line, *contact at Corner Station in three weeks*.'" Lynx stopped reading and closed her eyes in concentration, trying to solve the word puzzle from memory. "So the original message either read, '*Your training mission is top secret. Penetrate Farling home system to* acquire *Farling mind control drugs. Do not destroy this message. Contact at Corner Station in three weeks.'* or *'Top secret. Your training mission is to acquire Farling mind control drugs. Do not penetrate Farling home system. Contact at Corner Station in three weeks. Destroy this message.'* Wow, those are pretty different meanings," she concluded, opening her eyes and looking over at her partner. "We better line up the two halves of the paper to—what are you chewing on?"

A.P. held up his finger that Lynx should wait a minute and forced himself to swallow. "If it's not a big deal, I'd prefer if you ate all the secret messages from now on," he grumbled. "What were you just saying?"

"You ate your half?" Lynx asked in dismay. "But we needed to put the two pieces together to know what it means. Now I don't know if we're supposed to go to the Farling home system or just to one of their outer colonies on the tunnel network."

"We have three weeks to work it out," her partner replied complacently. "Perhaps we should do both."

"How can we both attempt to penetrate the Farling system and not attempt to penetrate the Farling home system?" Lynx demanded. Then it struck her like a thunderbolt that she was being tested again. The whole setup was too perfect. The director must have known that she would give the envelope to A.P. in the end, and there had probably been a trick to tearing it in half in exactly the right place. Maybe the message had been carefully torn in half before the envelope was even sealed! She had to give the EarthCent Intelligence professionals credit. They had stayed one step ahead of her all the way.

"If it was easy, they wouldn't need us," her partner replied jauntily. "So what are you going to tell the tunnel controller?"

"We'll start with the Farling outpost world, Seventy, since it's on the tunnel network," Lynx replied decisively. "I was there once years ago, and I'd be surprised if there's anything for sale in the Farling home system that isn't available on Seventy's orbital. If we can't buy drugs there, we'll trade for some goods that are attractive to the Farlings and see about going further. I don't know, though. The Farlings are pretty advanced, and I've never heard of anybody messing with them and getting away with it."

"Suits me fine," A.P. agreed. "I'm assuming you sleep in your chair on the bridge, so I'm going to go sack out in the cargo hold. I don't see any need to sync our schedules while we're in the tunnel, and we've both got plenty of material to study up on. Here's a display tab the Old Man gave me for you," he added, removing the device from a hidden pocket of his immaculately tailored jacket. "It's got some instructional videos and basic operational manuals for you to read through. I'll see you on the other side."

Lynx wasn't sure whether she was annoyed or relieved when her partner released his safety harness, kicked himself over to the ladder leading down into the hold, and disappeared without another word. It was true that the bridge of the two-man trader was cramped for living space and that the hold was still half-empty after loading the eclectic cargo, but she had planned to spend some time picking the senior agent's brain about his experiences. Maybe the rules prohibited sharing the details about former missions? She looked at the display tab A.P. had handed her and was about to check the contents when the comm system blinked to life.

"Stryx tunnel control to Prudence. Please supply your destination for queuing," the synthesized voice addressed her in unaccented English.

"Prudence to Stryx tunnel control. Our destination is Farling Seventy," Lynx responded.

"Will you be paying toll or sharing revenue?" the controller inquired politely. In the deal engineered through EarthCent eight years earlier, the Stryx gave human traders the option to go shares on their cargo profits rather than paying a cash toll. It was a money-losing proposition for the Stryx, but along with the elevators, it had made trade viable for the technologically backwards planet. Only a handful of humans understood what the Stryx were getting in return.

"Revenue sharing," Lynx replied from habit, though thinking about it, she wasn't sure it was a wise move operationally speaking, since it meant sharing the cargo manifest with the Stryx. The whole thing was conducted on the honor system, though human traders all had stories about some other guy who had been caught cheating by the seemingly omniscient AI. But on second thought, she doubted she had enough creds on her balance to pay the toll for real, and EarthCent Intelligence hadn't provided any cash funding. She double-checked that she had in fact reinserted the cargo management tab into its slot on the main console. "Transmitting cargo manifest now."

"You're queued for Farling Seventy, manipulator fields locking on," the controller reported after the longest pause Lynx could remember after transmitting a manifest. Later, she wasn't sure whether it was real or her imagination, but just as the stars smeared out to infinity and the Prudence began its violation of the human laws of physics, she swore she heard the tunnel controller comment, "Interesting cargo."

Five

The Prudence remained in the unique artificial universe of the Stryx tunnel for a little over seventy-five hours before emerging again in real space. During that time Lynx only saw her partner twice, both of these occasions coming as a result of her sticking her head into the cargo hold and looking for him. A.P. had tethered himself to a bulkhead cleat using a short cord tied around his ankle, and he was either sleeping or reading from his display tab as he floated in Zero-G. She couldn't tell which since his back was turned towards her. Lynx didn't know whether it was luck or sensitivity that had led her partner to restrict his visits to the lavatory corner on the bridge to while she was sleeping, but she was thankful in either case.

The comm came to life even before the stars stopped their post-tunnel wavering, and a creature resembling an armored beetle with an exaggerated number of teeth filled the main view screen. The native speech of the Farlings consisted of modulations on a high-bandwidth squeal produced by rubbing a specialized set of forelegs together, not unlike a mechanical version of an old FM radio transmitter, or amorous crickets. The trader implant Lynx had purchased at the same time as her ship handled the translation flawlessly.

"Seventy ground control to Prudence, Lynx Hedgehouse commanding. What is your destination?"

"Ground control, this is Lynx Edgehouse," she responded in irritation, stressing the 'E'. "Destination is Market Orbital."

"Identification unconfirmed," the insect replied. "Have you purchased Prudence from Lynx Hedgehouse?"

"It's Edgehouse, there is no Hedgehouse," Lynx replied through clenched teeth. She was beginning to wonder if there was some sort of mistake in the Stryx registry that would prove impossible to correct, forcing her to change her name.

"Hedgehouse deceased, Prudence now registered to Edgehouse," the ground controller confirmed in a bored whistle. "Since this is your first visit to Farling Seventy, we're transmitting the basic etiquette manual for primitives. You must complete the timed quiz at the end before you can dock at Market Orbital."

"Hedgehouse is not deceased," she argued in frustration. "Hedgehouse never existed. My name is Edgehouse, and I've been here before and passed your stupid quiz." She stiffened as she felt an impact and a hand gripping her shoulder, but it was just A.P., who had misdirected a dive from the ladder to his chair and was using Lynx as a pivot point.

"Stand by, Prudence," the beetle replied calmly, and turned to consult with somebody off screen.

"Nice trip," A.P. commented as he finally reached his seat and strapped on the safety harness. He glanced at the main viewer and took another second before asking, "Did you make it through the, uh, materials?"

"What?" Lynx replied reflexively, her mind fully occupied with the nonsense about her name. "Oh, yes, we can talk about that later," she added significantly, pointing her chin at the viewer.

"I just heard the end of that as I came in," A.P. admitted. "Is it possible that you have your name wrong?"

"Are you joking?" Lynx glared at her partner. "My name is my name. It's just this last month that everybody else is getting it wrong."

"It could be that the 'H' is pronounced silently where you grew up," A.P. mused. "If that's the case, you could go through life never knowing that it's actually Hedgehouse."

"It's Edgehouse!" Lynx practically shouted. "Edgehouse!"

A second beetle, larger than the first, entered the picture on the main screen and gazed at them through its multifaceted eyes. The new beetle's carapace was highlighted with emerald green, and it moved with the self-assurance of a bug long accustomed to command.

"I am senior controller G32FX," the flashy beetle rattled off its identification, undoubtedly for the record. "Junior controller K8CC reports a conflict between Prudence's transponder data and the self-identification of commander Lynx Edgehouse. All data conflicts must be resolved before Prudence can be authorized for docking or departure. Proceed to the designated quarantine area around the second planet."

Lynx bit her tongue and thought rapidly. Had the tech at Hawk's Orbital said something about upgrading her transponder to the new standard during her pit stop on the way to Earth a couple weeks ago? That could explain how EarthCent Intelligence, and now the Farlings, had gotten the spelling of her name wrong. She had a vague memory of a story about a trader running afoul of the bureaucratic Farlings and spending years fighting a charge of faking a cargo manifest, before abandoning his ship and fleeing back to Stryx space under an assumed identity. Lynx glanced at her partner, who as usual, showed no signs of being at all upset by the sudden turn of events.

"The 'H' is silent," she muttered at the view screen, feeling utterly defeated. "It's Hedgehouse, but the 'H' is silent. The controller might have recorded it improperly during my last visit."

"K8CC, check your records for confirmation," the senior controller instructed his subordinate. The smaller beetle tilted his head to the side for a moment, as if the files from previous years were stored in another part of his brain and had to be slid into place for processing.

"I have it," he reported a moment later, bringing his head back to even keel. "A Lynx Edgehouse commanding Prudence was here seven years ago and passed the etiquette test. Should I correct that record?"

"Do so," the senior controller instructed him. "Lynx Hedgehouse, the Prudence is cleared for docking at Market Orbital. If you remain in Farling space more than two cycles, you must report to the local head-tax office and apply for temporary residency status."

With that, the main viewer went blank, and Lynx was left alone with A.P. and what remained of her pride. She delayed a few minutes by setting course for Market Orbital at medium burn, and soon felt the tug of acceleration as her body sank gently into the cushioned seat.

"It really is Edgehouse," she finally said, not looking over at her partner. "There must be a problem with the ship's transponder, but no point in messing with it or we may never get out of Farling space."

"Is it safe to discuss the materials now?" A.P. asked her in response. Lynx was thankful he let the whole silent 'H' business pass without comment.

46

"The channel is closed," she replied, glancing at the status lights for confirmation. "We have as much privacy now as we'd have anywhere in space."

"Well, what did you learn?" her partner asked.

"I'm not exactly sure," Lynx replied. "The Ashenden material was very depressing, I wasn't quite sure if it was fact or fiction. I can't even imagine hiring an assassin, much less one who goes out and kills the wrong man."

"It was required reading for the intelligence service of the old British Empire at one point," A.P. informed her. "What else?"

"Well, I watched some of those old-fashioned movies, the pre-immersives," Lynx said. "I didn't really get the Bond ones. The female agents all kept getting killed, and the actor playing Bond changed so often that I could barely tell who was who. Then the Bourne movies seemed to be saying that the real enemy always turns out to be your boss."

"Did you read the training manuals from the Special Operations Executive?" her partner inquired.

"Yes, but it was all so outdated," Lynx complained in frustration. "World War Two was just twenty years or so after the Ashenden war, so we're still talking about more than a hundred and fifty years ago. And it all applied to humans spying on humans in old nation states, using obsolete weapons and communications technologies that any AI could crack in its sleep. Is this really supposed to be training, or is it a test to see whether or not we're serious?"

"Your guess is as good as mine," A.P. replied with a shrug. "Anyway, our orders are clear enough. We're supposed to find out if the Farlings have been targeting humanity with their drug engineering and to make sure we're back at Corner Station in three weeks, no, seventeen days now, where we'll be contacted."

"Doesn't it bother you that our employers seem so hands-off?" Lynx asked cautiously. "I mean, other than the oddball cargo, their entire investment in this mission was limited to two contacts, a meeting, and that envelope thing that came without instructions for getting it opened!"

"So what do you plan to do when we dock at Market Orbital?" her partner asked, ignoring her question.

"Check out the market conditions, try to make some advantageous trades. Keep our ears open," she suggested.

"That's all good, but I was hoping for something more active," A.P. replied. "I was thinking about hitting the bars and spreading some creds around."

"Whose creds?" Lynx asked sourly, though deep inside, she already knew the answer to that one. Then her natural suspicion took over. "Are you a drinker, Malloy?"

"I guess I can handle my alcohol," the agent acknowledged with a bemused expression. "Of course, that's the whole point of the program, to keep your head while others lose theirs."

"How about trading?" Lynx asked. "Do you have any experience in business, or is it all spy work with you?"

"My career prior to taking this job was primarily in supervisory positions," A.P. informed her, relapsing into the superior tone that had bothered her when she first met him. "I worked with dozens of alien species on highly sensitive assignments. In fact, I was pretty much the go-to guy in the organization. But I've never done any trading or selling because I just wasn't in that end of the business."

"Alright, we have a few hours to kill, so I'll give you a crash course," Lynx told him. She figured it couldn't hurt to show-off her own skills a little. Maybe her partner had answered the way he did specifically because he wanted to see what she would do, but this whole apprenticeship relationship was for the birds. "I don't want to leave the bridge while we're in the shipping lanes, so you go down to the hold and bring back a couple of different boxes, though it doesn't really matter which. On second thought, stick with the boxes that are already open, because there are some buyers who will pay more for factory sealed cases, even with the identical contents."

A.P. unstrapped his safety harness and launched himself at the ladder, scoring a direct hit this time, and then disappearing below. Lynx undid her own four-point restraint, activated her magnetic cleats, and shuffled over to one of the bridge's storage lockers. She keyed in her personal security code and opened the door slowly, not remembering if she had packed everything for Zero-G. The locker contained her basic trading kit for open-air markets, including a blanket, a Stryx mini-register, a roll of brown wrapping paper and several balls of twine. She took the blanket and the mini-register, leaving the packing materials, balance scales, and a dagger that she always wore on the tech-ban worlds. The dagger was also useful for cutting the twine.

A box preceded her partner out of the ladder-way, and Lynx was about to yell at him for setting an object in motion on a live bridge, when she saw it was tethered by a short cord to the wrist which appeared soon after. Then A.P. himself came back into view, holding another box by a cord that had been tied around it to keep the flaps closed. He had taken her literally and selected two of the cartons that looked like they had ended up in the container by mistake.

"First things first," Lynx declared as she snapped out the blanket. The engines had already taken the ship up to cruising speed and they were coasting towards the orbital, so there was nothing to hold the blanket to the deck. She placed the mini-register in the middle and keyed it on, activating its magnetic base. Now the blanket was secured, but the edges were up off the deck, making the whole thing look like the blossom of some weird, rectangular flower.

"Activate your cleats and sit cross-legged on your side of the blanket," Lynx advised him, while moving to do the same herself. "There's still enough magnetic attraction through the sides of the cleats to hold you in place." In less than a minute, the two agents sat across from each other on the blanket. A.P. still held one box, the other remained tethered to his wrist.

"Do you want the boxes?" he asked hopefully, undoubtedly feeling a little over-encumbered.

"Not yet," Lynx replied. "Do you understand the significance of the blanket in trading?"

"Seems a little old-fashioned," her partner responded without directly answering the question.

"The blanket is the trader's real estate," Lynx explained. "When you set up to trade in a crowded market, you need a way to declare what belongs to you, so that shoppers will know who to bargain with, and other traders won't walk off with your goods. When you don't have a booth or a shop, the blanket is your territory. I've traded in hundreds of different markets in my life, and nobody has ever stepped on my blanket. It just isn't done."

"Blanket is sacred," A.P. said. "Got it. Is that an altar in the middle?"

"A what?" Lynx asked in surprise. "Do you think I'm running some kind of cult here? It's a Stryx mini-register."

"I guess I've never seen one," her partner replied. "I've never been much for shopping. What's it do?"

"What's it do?" Lynx repeated in disbelief. She was about to tell A.P. to either stop fooling around or to get off her ship when she remembered that he was just testing her. "It processes incoming payments over the Stryxnet. It can't initiate payments beyond its current value because it's not authorized to tap other sources, like a full register. It's essentially an interface for a programmable Stryx coin, so we can accept payments from any of the currency containers it recognizes. Traders obviously prefer barter when we're doing business with each other, but for an odd lots cargo that we'll be selling in the market, it's mainly a cash business."

"So let me make sure I have this straight," A.P. deadpanned. "Somebody who wants to buy from us can offer up a currency container, like their own programmable Stryx cred, and the mini-register will deduct the value from their container and add it to ours?"

"That's it, but unlike a full register, it can't draw from other credit sources," Lynx recapped the limitations. "The only way to get money out of the mini-register is to pull the programmable Stryx coin and spend it with a vendor who accepts them."

"That's fine," her partner said magnanimously. "How much of the market business usually goes through the mini-register?"

"Depends on the location and the customers," Lynx replied. "On stations, a lot of people carry a programmable coin just to avoid pockets full of change, but the farther you get from the stations, the more trade is carried out in local coinage or nonprogrammable Stryx creds. Some traders get by without a mini-register and let that part of the business walk away, but it wasn't that expensive, and it acts sort of like a portable safe since it won't disgorge the coin without the pass code."

"What's the pass code?" A.P. asked.

"That's on a need-to-know basis," his partner replied, and hastened to change the subject. "Now what did you bring up for trade goods?"

"This box is supposed to contain tools," agent Malloy responded, indicating the carton in his lap. "The other one here just has 'Kitchen' written on it."

"Pass me the kitchen box," Lynx said with a sigh. There was no question left in her mind that their cargo was mixed in with somebody's household goods, and whoever the stuff belonged to, she only hoped they had good taste and better moving insurance, because it was way too late to send the stuff back. A.P. untied the cord from his wrist and gently pushed the box over to Lynx. She picked open the knot where the string circled the box and began looking through the contents.

"Any idea what this is?" her partner asked, holding up an object with a wooden handle as long as his forearm that was attached to a curiously shaped black metal head. One end of the chunk of metal featured a round, silvery surface, about the size of a fifty cred piece, and the other end terminated in what looked like a curved wedge with a triangle cut out of the middle. A.P. gave it a tentative swing. "I'm guessing it's a primitive mace."

"It's a carpenter's hammer," Lynx told him after glancing up. "I take it you haven't spent any time on colony worlds where they build shelters with wood and

52

nails. You use the shiny part to drive the nails into the wood and the claw part to take them out."

"Interesting," A.P. commented, sticking the handle of the hammer under one knee to keep it from floating off. "I thought wood was only used for expensive furniture and musical instruments."

"Just on the stations and orbitals," Lynx replied. "On planets where it's grown, humanoids use wood for everything, including adding fiber to food and burning it to keep warm."

"Weird," her partner commented, removing a boxy silver object about as big as his palm from the box. A small tab protruded from one end, and he began to pull it, exposing a narrow strip of metallic yellow tape with numbers on it. "And this?"

"It's a measuring tape," Lynx replied in frustration as she looked up again. "Haven't you ever spent any time around construction?"

"Just in space," A.P. admitted. He looked like he was going to say something further, but then he replaced the tape in the box and continued shifting the hand-tools around, looking for something else of interest.

"I can't believe it!" Lynx exclaimed, drawing a flat wooden case from her carton. She flipped open the lid and began to examine the contents, removing a spoon from its velvet resting place and squinting at the markings. "Sterling silver! I thought this case looked familiar because I saw a set just like this at an antique cutlery fair a few months ago. It needs a good shine, but it could be worth thousands of creds if it's by a quality maker."

"How come you get the good stuff and I'm stuck with these glass containers of little spears?" her partner complained, holding up a baby food jar in each hand.

"The smooth ones are the nails I told you about, the twisty ones are screws," Lynx explained patiently, the silver having greatly improved her mood. "It's all useful for working with wood, and while none of it is very valuable, it's good barter stuff for a colony world. Look, I'll give you this silver teaspoon for everything in your box."

"Deal," A.P. said, sticking the two jars and the hammer back in his carton and folding the flaps to stay closed.

"What's wrong with you?" Lynx asked, staring at her partner in open-mouthed amazement. "It's bad enough you don't know what a mini-register is for, but now you're going to tell me you've never bartered for anything either? Never accept the first bid. I don't care if somebody offers you a spaceship for a bottle of wine. Maybe there's an emperor around the corner offering a fleet for just one glass."

"I've bartered," agent Malloy defended himself, "I just don't want any of this stuff for anything. The silver spoon is as good as a silver coin."

"That's not the point!" Lynx exploded. "You can't make a living as a trader if you value your goods according to whether they fit your personal needs. Do you think we should give away all that dog food just because we don't have a dog? The idea is to always maximize the value of your cargo, and that depends on figuring out what it's worth to the other party."

"Alright, I get it. So give me two teaspoons," A.P. replied with infuriating calm.

"Forget it," Lynx hissed, setting the flatware chest aside and closing up the box. "I'll do all the trading for now and you just keep your ears open and try to look good."

"I do look good, don't I?" her partner replied complacently.

Six

"Blythe, Clive, thank you for coming," Kelly said as she rose from the couch to greet her guests. "I just finished feeding Samuel, so you have great timing."

"You know I'm permanently in your debt," Clive replied, fingering the Key of Eff that hung around his neck. "If you're ready to ask for something in return, you'll be doing me a favor."

"Subject to approval by the management," Blythe interjected, hooking her arm through Clive's.

"It's nothing like that, exactly." Kelly hesitated, as if she was in no hurry to explain further. "I could use a cup of tea. How about you two?"

"Tea would be nice," Blythe agreed.

"It's a little late for tea," Clive observed. "Is Joe around? I missed his beer while we were away on the grand InstaSitter tour of the stations."

"Joe will be joining us in a minute, he's reading a bedtime story with Dorothy," Kelly replied, then turned to Blythe. "Could you hold Samuel while I get the tea?"

"Has he burped yet?" Blythe asked suspiciously, proving that you don't become the co-owner of the galaxy's most successful babysitting service without being on the ball.

"Not technically, no," Kelly admitted, holding the baby suspended halfway between them. "But he rarely spits up in any case, and I'll loan you my towel."

"You should really relax with the baby for a few minutes after feeding him," Blythe suggested, backpedalling away from the extended infant. "I know where the tea things are, I'll be back in a minute."

"I'm not afraid of a little regurgitation," Clive declared bravely. "I'll take him if you want."

Kelly glanced at the kitchen and whispered to Clive, "That's not the point. Donna asked me to get Blythe to hold Samuel whenever the opportunity presents itself. Ever since the two of you got married, she's become obsessed with the topic of grandchildren. Hadn't you noticed?"

"It's a bit hard not to notice," Clive whispered back in amusement. "When we went over for dinner last night, I thought my mother-in-law was practicing some sort of alien martial arts because I'd never seen or heard of knitting before. It turned out she was making baby socks, and when Blythe asked if they were for Samuel, Donna said she was preparing for a grandchild."

"Hey, what are you whispering to my wife about?" Joe cried in mock anger as he entered the living room. "You've got one of your own, or has she wised up and left you already?"

"Clive was just telling me how much he missed your beer, Joe," Kelly told her husband. She sat back down with the baby. "Blythe is in the kitchen getting the two of us tea, so maybe you can draw a couple of glasses for the two of you?"

"Come along and carry," Joe ordered the younger man, and the two of them headed down a deck to the brew room. "Sorry if I seem a bit out of it tonight. I took care of Dorothy most of the day to give Kelly a chance to relax with the baby. Eight-year-old girls have way too much energy."

"Speaking of energy, where's Beowulf?" the ex-mercenary asked, playing off the giant canine's famous laziness. The old war dog had successfully trained Clive to serve as a source of snacks, so it was strange that he hadn't put in a showing yet.

"He's probably sleeping under the tap, dreaming that the valve fails and it starts dripping," Joe replied. "Killer's been hiding down here a lot the last few months, he's always been spooked by infants. I think he isn't comfortable with how helpless they are. He stayed away from Dorothy until she could crawl."

Joe's prediction proved correct, and Beowulf was indeed stretched out on his side in front of the current keg, his massive head directly under the tap. When the men approached, he opened one eye, whacked his tail on the deck a couple times, and then waited for further developments.

"Do you know why the ambassador invited us over?" Clive asked.

"Yup, but it's a secret," Joe replied with a grin, retrieving a couple of glasses and a pitcher from the sink rack. "Here, you fill the glasses and then I'll hand you the pitcher. I'm betting Blythe will want to switch over from tea when she hears what Kelly has to say."

"Sounds serious," Clive replied. He took a glass from Joe and held it under the tap, pulling down the handle. The ex-mercenary stood awkwardly, his feet straddling the giant dog's head, but he didn't spill a single drop as he hot-swapped the glasses under the flow. Joe whistled in admiration as Beowulf shot the man a look of disgust. Clive winked at the dog and asked Joe, "Can you tell me if it's official ambassadorial business?"

Joe took the full glass from Clive, handed him the empty pitcher, and watched as Clive repeated the hot-swap operation to perfection. "I think I better leave all of the details to Kelly," he replied after a pause, and took the second glass from Clive. "You'll understand after you've been married for a while. I'll see you upstairs."

Joe started up the improvised stairway with a full glass in each hand, and Clive shut the tap and waited for the dripping to stop before removing the pitcher. "Sorry, old friend," he muttered to the dog, feeling guilty over pulling off the operation so cleanly. As Clive turned away from the keg, Beowulf lifted up his head, just enough to catch the man's trailing leg and produce a stumble. A glass worth of beer sloshed over the brim of the pitcher onto the clean metal decking, which pitched towards a drain below the keg. The dog was ready and waiting, and his tongue began lapping overtime as he prevented a single drop from going to waste.

"Sounds like he got you," Joe called down the stairs without turning around to look.

"Yeah," Clive admitted. "Should I top off again?"

"No. One beer a night is his limit," Joe answered sardonically.

The two men arrived back in the living room just as Blythe emerged from the galley with a teapot and two mugs. Kelly had never been a fan of china teacups with their dainty handles and saucers, and truth be told, she was really a coffee person. But she liked her coffee strong and worried that it wasn't good for the baby while nursing, so she shifted to herbal tea rather than watering down her favorite beverage.

Kelly eased Samuel into the cushion-lined hand-woven basket she had received from the Hadads as a baby present. The baby pursed his little lips, but he didn't open his eyes, and if he wasn't sleeping, he had a great career ahead of him as an actor. Although it was warmer in the converted ice-harvester that served as their home than in the rest of Mac's Bones, she covered Samuel with a little quilt.

"What I'm going to talk about here today is top secret," Kelly began, blushing at the pretentiousness of her own words. "I mean, if we actually had any secrets it would be top secret, except of course from the Stryx, since Libby is always listening anyway. But it doesn't mean that the Stryx approve or disapprove, though unofficially, they think it's a good idea. Not this part, I mean, which I haven't even discussed with Libby, though she could probably guess what I'm going to say because she's good at that sort of thing."

"Kelly's a little out of practice talking to adults," Joe explained to Blythe and Clive, both of whom wore similar looks of incomprehension as Kelly paused to sip her tea. "Just hang in there and she'll hit her stride."

"Was I going off point again?" Kelly asked, reviewing her words. "Oops, I guess I did, which is a shame, since I actually prepared for this because I really wanted to get it right. It's just that somebody, well, the High Priest of Kasil, told me that finding the right person for a job was the hardest part of her own duties, and my experience in hiring anybody is nonexistent. I practically had to beg EarthCent for Aisha, and I probably wouldn't have gotten her if Jeeves hadn't already picked her for ulterior motives."

"Uh, Kelly?" Joe said, interrupting his wife's exposition of her internal thought process. "Why not explain it to them just like you explained it to me?"

"Oh, right," Kelly replied, visibly pulling herself into focus. "EarthCent has decided we need to start spying, and I have a seat on the Earth Intelligence Committee."

"EEK?" Blythe guessed, or perhaps it was her honest reaction.

"You see, we're both on the same page," Kelly continued enthusiastically. "We've already started recruiting agents, using an actor as the director, but the committee agrees that we need to get a real agency head in place as soon as possible. I've been tasked to find somebody for the job."

"Do I get to run everything?" Blythe asked.

"Yes, under the committee's supervision," Kelly replied, before she realized she hadn't even offered the job yet.

"How often does the committee meet?" Clive inquired.

"Well, just once so far," Kelly confessed. "Before the meeting, we exchanged a few notes. Basically, EarthCent roped in the ambassadors who had asked about starting an intelligence agency to serve as the committee members. EarthCent's unelected president hired the actors on Earth to give us a running start with recruiting."

"Is it going to be funded any better than the embassy?" Clive asked, having heard all about EarthCent's precarious financial situation from his wife.

Blythe looked at her husband with a bemused smile. "Why do you think she's recruiting us?"

"Oh," Clive replied, and drained his glass. Then he reached for the pitcher and poured himself another.

"I'll admit the committee is counting on the new director to help fund the agency," Kelly replied. "But we're hoping that by recruiting agents who already own their own ships, it won't be that expensive."

"I'm not worried about the expense." Blythe shrugged off Kelly's financial concerns. "If you give me a free hand, I'll have the agency running at a profit within a year. My sister and Tinka can handle InstaSitter, and we have more money than we know what to do with. But I think it will work better if we make Clive the head and I just handle the management side."

"I thought you'd want to be in charge," Kelly said, looking at the younger woman in surprise.

"She will be," Clive muttered, drawing a sympathetic look from Joe.

"I'm just twenty-one and I look like I was brought up in a convent," Blythe stated flatly. "Clive is twenty-eight and he looks like a thirty-five-year-old ex-mercenary. Appearances matter in a job like this."

"Always nice to be recognized for my unique talents," Clive observed dryly. "But who exactly gets to see the director of the agency?"

"Agents, eventually," Blythe replied, her mind racing ahead. "And the heads of alien agencies, though that's less important since they probably can't tell a young human face from an old one. Even Kelly's committee would be more inclined to put their trust in you rather than me. It's just natural."

"As the EarthCent military attaché, I have to agree with Blythe," Joe said, invoking his honorary title. "Come to think of it, aren't military attachés expected to be spies?"

61

"You can spy as much as you want as long as you're home to help keep an eye on Dorothy," Kelly told him. "Oops, I guess that's not really my call now, assuming the two of you are accepting the job."

"Were you planning this when you sent me to convince Aisha that EarthCent needed an intelligence agency a couple of weeks ago?" Blythe asked.

"No, and the truth is, I never expected the home office would act on the request, especially not this fast," Kelly replied. "I suspect there's something the EarthCent president isn't sharing with the rest of us, but maybe you'll figure that out and tell me."

"Where are Aisha and Paul?" Blythe inquired, as if she had just noticed they weren't present. "Are we supposed to keep this secret from them?"

"They're at a reception for the new Vergallian ambassador," Joe replied. "You're going to have to start keeping secrets at some point, so you may as well get into practice."

"I don't think Aisha would want to know too much in any case," Kelly added.

"What about guidelines?" Clive asked. "I assume that EarthCent wants an intelligence service on the general principle that all of the other species either have a dedicated spy service or a military equivalent. But we're never going to catch up with the kind of general information you can get just by asking a Stryx librarian, or even a tutor bot for that matter. Joe and I have plenty of experience with the kind of tactical intelligence that military units need in the field, but most of that involves talking with the locals or studying images taken from space."

"I've done my share of hiding in the bushes and counting heads," Joe added.

"The committee is working on the guidelines," Kelly reassured them. "We should have a draft at the next meeting. But I can tell you based on the previous discussion that we're more interested in big-picture issues for now."

"For example?" Blythe prompted.

Kelly took another sip of tea and resisted the urge to ask Libby to reel off the contents of her committee meeting. Even ignoring the fact that EarthCent hadn't paid for encryption, Libby listened to everything that went on in the embassy office. Kelly was officially on maternity leave, but she had snuck into the office in the early morning hours for the meeting, since the arbitrary Union Station time in the human sections ran nine hours behind the clock back at headquarters on Earth. Now that she thought of it, in addition to owning the communications network and listening in at her office, the end user license agreement for her diplomatic implant allowed the Stryx to eavesdrop anyway.

"To the best of my memory, there was the suggestion that we start keeping track of the military capabilities and alliances of the other species," Kelly began, ticking items off on her fingers. "Then there was the whole subject of commercial espionage, including the point that what we don't know might hurt us. Uh, somebody mentioned data mining, which I thought was a pretty good idea since there's no shortage of data in the galaxy. I guess that would mean hiring some analysts. Counterintelligence came up, though I'm not sure that's really something to focus on since I doubt we could stop anybody and I'm not sure what we have to hide. Oh, and there's quite a bit of concern about mind control, whether through telepathy or drugs."

"That really covers the gamut," Clive commented, but he looked singularly undaunted by the assignment, as if he'd successfully completed more difficult tasks in the past. "And as the new species in the galaxy, I guess we'll stumble into every one of the potential holes at least once before we really understand what's going on. Did you have any special concerns of your own, Mrs. Ambassador?"

Kelly took a self-conscious glance at the ceiling before answering. "I sort of brought up the fact that the maps we get from the Stryx seem to be more about keeping us out of trouble then opening up the galaxy."

"How so?" Blythe asked. "Have you talked it over with Libby? Why don't we just ask her?"

"Oh, I don't think that's necessary," Kelly backtracked rapidly, but Blythe had already made up her mind.

"Libby?" Blythe asked, without looking anywhere in particular. "Are the maps that come with the Stryx ship controllers accurate?"

"Absolutely," the Stryx station librarian declared without hesitation. "Hello, Clive. Hi, Joe. I was a bit puzzled by your suspicion about our maps, Kelly, but I didn't feel it was my place to comment without being asked."

"Space monsters?" Kelly inquired skeptically. "That's the sort of thing people used to put on maps of Earth when they didn't have a clue what was really there. I know the Stryx have thoroughly explored this galaxy at one time or another, so what's with all the monsters on the map?"

"I believe you are referring to the Floppsies," Libby replied, rather stiffly. "Just because they prefer to be left alone doesn't make them monsters. The Floppsies could have taken over this galaxy when they first arrived, but they believe deeply in giving other species a chance to thrive."

"You see?" Blythe said. "That's one item off our plate. Thanks, Libby."

"You know that the Stryx, uh, exaggerate for our own good at times," Kelly cautioned Blythe.

"Libby wouldn't lie to me about something like space monsters," Blythe declared with the confidence of youth. "Anyway, Clive can check the Effterii maps if you're unconvinced. His ship doesn't have a Stryx controller."

"Getting back to the point, the two of you have agreed that Clive will accept the job as the EarthCent Intelligence Director and Blythe will handle the management tasks from the shadows, right?" Joe prompted.

"Sounds good to me," Blythe replied. Clive nodded manfully and finished off his second glass of beer. "When do we start meeting the agents recruited by actors who no doubt were hired through an actor's agent?"

"The committee agreed to stop referring to the entertainment industry professionals using job descriptions that overlap with the intelligence business," Kelly informed her. "It was just getting too confusing, like that last question that I'm still trying to figure out."

"Fair enough," Blythe replied. "When do we start meeting our employees?"

"I think there are only the two of them so far, and EarthCent's home office dispatched them on a training mission to Farling space."

"Not good," Blythe said. "What do you think, Mr. Director?"

"We should probably chase them down with the Effterii and pull them back before they get into trouble," Clive said. "I doubt the wisdom of sending untrained agents recruited by, uh, entertainment industry professionals, to go practice on one of the more advanced species who keep most of their empire off the tunnel network."

"We'd like to see a copy of their orders, if that's possible," Blythe told Kelly. "And if the embassy doesn't have anything major coming up, I think it would be a big help to sponsor an intelligence trade show."

"You want us to sponsor a trade show for spies?" Kelly asked. "Isn't that just begging for trouble?"

"It's more of a statement as I see it," Blythe replied calmly. "And a big trade show is always good for the station economy. I'll bet you that my mom and Libby saved the guest list from the Earth Exposition you did a couple years ago, so you could notify all of those attendees to start. Once the diplomats tell their spies and the spies tell their suppliers, I bet the vendor space will rent out in a jiffy."

"But what do we gain if you're right?" Kelly asked doubtfully. "A statement that we're ready to start spying on everybody?"

"I want them to know that we're open for business," Blythe replied. "Maybe we can carve out a niche as a middleman while we're building up our own resources. We have to be open-minded about this. The Tharks have a great business as the middlemen of the galactic business community recording contracts and deeds."

"She's got a point," Clive agreed. "If humanity has one thing going for us, it's that compared to all of the older species, we haven't had any time to make enemies. Well, that and the fact that we still have a lot of energy and enthusiasm for travel. That's what makes treasure-hunting possible, the reason why all the good stuff wasn't dug up millions of years ago. You give the average alien a treasure map to a lost city on the other side of the galaxy and he'll put it in a frame and hang it on the wall. You give the same map to a human and he'll sell his house to buy some wreck of a spaceship to go there, without even checking if the planet still exists."

"I've been to a number of military trade shows, Kel, and if Blythe is willing to spend some cash on spy gear, it's a great way to see the latest products and compare prices," Joe observed. "Besides, you wouldn't believe the free samples some of the alien vendors give out at these things."

"Alright, I'll tell Aisha to get started on it," Kelly replied. "But don't blame me if the aliens see right through us."

"Oh, they see through us already, Aunty Kelly," Blythe assured the ambassador. "When it comes to intelligence, we're like Sammy there. We have to crawl before we can walk, and it's going to take a while to master that crawling thing."

Seven

"What is that, some sort of laser weapon?" A.P. asked hopefully when Lynx showed him the impressive barrel lens for her latest barter acquisition. He had just returned to the trading deck after an extended reconnaissance of the orbital, a mission suggested by his partner, who had declared him to be worse than useless at bartering.

"It's a telephoto lens for my new camera," Lynx replied. She remounted the lens on the single reflex body and admired the smooth operation of the adjustment rings. "A hundred years ago on Earth, no self-respecting family would be without one. Then the technology changed and all of a sudden you couldn't give them away. A decade or two ago somebody figured out that alien collectors would buy cameras as a form of ancient industrial art, and then some forensic entrepreneur on Earth began manufacturing film for them again. Now they're a huge fad with the arts crowd. I have a friend on Echo Station who makes a decent living photographing weddings and special events. Of course, it takes forever to see how the pictures came out because you have to send them back to Earth for developing."

"I don't get it," A.P. objected. "Pretty much everything that walks upright can save an image just by looking at something. You have a pretty good implant yourself, so what's the point of a machine that only takes pictures?"

"You do realize that humans didn't have implants before the Stryx opened Earth," Lynx reminded him. "And photographs are different from stored images. It's a chemical process that starts with capturing the light and goes through several steps before the results are transferred to special paper. Somebody who's good with one of these things can create real art."

"Do you even know how to use it?" A.P. asked.

"I'm no artist, but I can make it work," Lynx replied. "Plus, I got two rolls of film in the deal and the date code is good for another eight cycles. Besides, it wasn't just a good trade, it's something we can use for, uh, you know."

"I know?" her partner asked.

"Surveillance," Lynx mouthed the word.

"Oh, like in the training materials," A.P. acknowledged. "Well, you're not the only one who's been productive today."

"Find anything interesting?" Lynx asked, glancing around to see if anybody was paying attention to them. The agents had discussed operational security and concluded that as long as they didn't use words like "spying" or "secret plans," it wouldn't be risky to discuss their work in public places if they kept it vague.

"I visited all of the bars on the orbital for oxygen/nitrogen breathers," A.P. reported proudly. "Assuming you picked up a little hard cash to go with that antique, I'm ready for some serious drinking. It turns out the Farlings dedicated a whole deck on this orbital to servicing travelers, and you wouldn't believe some of the offers I turned down during my investigations. But there are also a few hole-in-the-wall bars right below the docking ring that were nowhere near as noisy and where the customers looked more like locals than tourists. What's your call?"

Lynx grimaced at yet another multiple-choice test, but she replied confidently. "We'll hit the dive bars. I don't want to spend a lot of money on drinks for the sake of a conversation I can't even hear."

A.P. helped Lynx repack the remaining inventory into boxes, and he saw that she had successfully disposed of most of the stock he'd helped her carry in a few hours earlier. Lynx had decided to start the business part of their mission with the tough stuff, the items that wouldn't be easy to get rid of, such as the old clothes, ping pong balls, and used household items that had apparently come their way by mistake. There weren't too many humans flowing through Market Orbital, but a good thirty percent of the crowds were humanoid species. The used household items had mainly brought small change, but it got them out of the hold and it would pay for a few rounds of drinks. Before folding up the blanket, Lynx pulled a pair of good leather shoes and an old iron frying pan out of an unsold items box and placed them at the front of the space she had occupied for six hours.

"Not worth carrying back?" A.P. inquired. It amused Lynx that a man who was so curious about everything related to business could be so bad at it.

"Trader's tithe," she explained. "I'd call today moderately successful, so I'm leaving these for the gleaners, the poor people who end up stuck on a place like this. If whoever takes the stuff can use it, that's great, and if they can't, they can barter for a meal or a blanket to roll up in at night. These orbitals aren't like the Stryx stations, where as long as you have your sanity, you can always get back on your feet. You go down and out in a place like this and it's the end of the line."

"So it's charity," A.P. interpreted her words. "I saw plenty of biologicals pan-handling on the entertainment deck, but I didn't see anybody making contributions. You're a good woman, partner."

For the first time since they met, Lynx actually felt something like warmth for the senior agent, who she had come to regard as a sort of unwanted babysitter. Maybe when the apprenticeship period was over they could explore another type of relationship, but for the time being, she was maintaining a strict separation between her personal and professional lives.

After a quick stop back at the Prudence to drop off the leftover trade goods and the antique camera, Lynx and A.P. headed out for one of the nearby bars he'd scouted. There was no day/night lighting cycle on Market Orbital, the place was always open so it didn't matter what clock you were using. The bartender was a scruffy-looking Horten who didn't even bother wearing an isolation suit, a sure sign that the alien had just stopped caring. He barely changed colors when Agent Malloy reached over the bar to tap his shoulder.

"What you want, bub?" the Horten snarled. Even though her commercial translation implant tended to miss the emotional nuances when aliens spoke, Lynx could tell that there was no real rancor in his tone. It was more like he was stuck playing a part in a play for which he hadn't intended to audition.

"Bottle of your finest cheap stuff and two glasses, human consumption," A.P. requested. Lynx thought it was an interesting formulation, and then she wondered why her partner had taken it onto himself to order for both of them. Lynx also realized that she was hungry, and after days of subsisting mainly on nutrient squeeze tubes, she was ready for some solid food if she could find something that wouldn't kill her. But the bartender was already pushing a dusty bottle of vodka across the bar, along with two glasses.

"Six creds," the Horten stated. "That cheap enough for you, big spender?"

"Thank you," Lynx inserted herself into the dialogue, producing a ten-cred piece and sliding it across the bar. She kept a finger on top of the coin and gently interrogated the bartender. "You wouldn't know where a human could order some solid food around here, would you?"

The bartender pointedly ignored A.P. as he eyed the coin and took Lynx's measure, in that order. His skin turned a reddish purple, which having traded with plenty of Hortens, Lynx associated with greed. Greed is good, she said to herself.

"I might know a place to call, does take-out for humanoids. I know the Drazens and Vergallians eat the stuff," he replied, reaching for the coin. "Can't guarantee it's not poison for humans, but it's your best bet."

"Does this place have a name?" Lynx asked, keeping her finger on the ten creds.

"Panda Pagoda," the Horten grunted out the unfamiliar syllables.

Lynx broke into a smile and took her finger off the coin. "That's great, best Chinese chain in the galaxy. Can I link your comm and ping them?"

"All the take-out places on the orbital work through the menu tabs," the bartender replied, looking a good deal more cheerful as he swept up the coin. He reached under the bar and came up with a cracked tab that looked like it had never been cleaned, but the screen was live. "They're pretty fast, around fifteen minutes for deliveries."

"Thanks again," Lynx said. Then she told the device, "Panda Pagoda." The screen blinked once or twice and then came up with the standard menu that she could have ordered from in her sleep. "It's on me, Malloy. What can I get you?"

"I had something while I was wandering around," A.P. replied vaguely. "Just suit yourself and I'll fuel up on the good stuff." To accentuate his point, he twisted the lid off the vodka bottle and filled both glasses to the rim. Then he downed them, one after another, thumping the bar with his fist after each drink. "That hit the spot," he declared. "I think I could live on this stuff for months."

"When you asked for two glasses, I sort of assumed that one of them was for me," Lynx complained, but she had to admit to herself it was an impressive display. If he wasn't dead drunk in a half an hour, it could be a useful talent for a spy. After a quick tap and a swipe, the menu flashed, "Order accepted. Delivery to your location in 2.436." Lynx didn't have a clue what time base the orbital was on, but the last digit was cycling continually and the second to last digit changed every few seconds, so it wouldn't be a long wait.

"I was just cleaning the glass for you," A.P. told her. He poured a refill and lowered his voice before he spoke again. "Best way to poison somebody is to coat the inside of a glass with the toxins. It's in the training material, somewhere."

"Oh, uh, thanks I guess," Lynx replied as she lifted a glass and took a little sip. "Yuck, tastes like medicine," she said. "I would have paid for a bottle of Scotch if they have one."

"Lots of impurities in Scotch," her partner replied. "Vodka is the safest drink."

"Safest drink?" Lynx asked in surprise. "None of it is safe. That's sort of the whole point."

"Why don't we move to a table while there's an opening, unless you wanted to eat standing at the bar," A.P. suggested, at the same time indicating the doorway with a tilt of his head. "You never know when a place like this will get crowded."

Lynx stole a look at the new arrival as she followed her partner to a small metal table protruding from the wall. The woman's dress didn't leave much to the imagination and she was making for A.P. like a homing missile. Agent Malloy was still fidgeting with the control slider to adjust the height of the seats and the tabletop when the newcomer strutted up.

"Hey, big boy," she said, batting her eyelash extensions at A.P. "I'm running a bit low on fuel here. How 'bout sharing?"

Lynx watched in amazement as her partner refilled his glass and pushed it to the end of the table. The orbital tramp downed the drink in a gulp and smacked her lips.

"Plenty more where that came from," A.P. leered, and patted the bench seat with his hand. The woman didn't hesitate to accept the invitation. Agent Malloy retrieved the glass and filled it to the brim, but this time, he didn't rush to slide it over. Instead, he cupped the glass in both hands, winked in exaggerated fashion, and said, "Of course, nothing is free in this world."

"You don't have to explain the facts of life to me, sport," the woman replied, reaching over and retrieving the brimming glass. For the second time, she drained the contents in one go, causing Lynx to sample her own drink again. It was high-proof alcohol all right, and the glass was more than double the size of a standard human shot. She felt a surge of sympathy for any woman who could toss the stuff back like their table guest.

"I'm A.P. Malloy and this is Lynx," her partner introduced them. Normally, Lynx would expect to be introduced as Captain Edgehouse, but either A.P. was preparing an elaborate lie to make himself look good, or he just didn't want to reopen the controversy about the pronunciation of her name.

"A.P., I like that," the woman replied, adding a husky laugh. "I'm Chance, just plain Chance, as in, you're welcome to take one."

"Hi, Chance," Lynx said, feeling she had better join the conversation before the two of them began undressing each other right across from her, not that the woman had far to go to complete the process. "I've got some Chinese food coming, Panda Pagoda, and I know I ordered more than I can eat."

"Uh, thanks. I'm alright," Chance responded, turning to straighten an imaginary out-of-place hair behind Malloy's ear. "Me and gorgeous here have our own dinner plans. Don't we?"

"I think I can go one more on credit," A.P. replied, smiling wickedly as he refilled the glass yet again. Lynx began to understand why he had called for a bottle as Chance drained it as quickly as her first two. He retrieved the glass from Chance, poured it full again, and this time he faked handing it to her before raising it to his own lips.

Lynx gritted her teeth and forced herself to down a gulp from her own drink, almost gagging in the process. When she opened her eyes again and looked at the glass, it was still two-thirds full. She wondered if the bartender had any beer back there, but it was doubtful. Unlike liquor and wine, only a few species would touch the carbonated Earth beverage, which didn't travel well in any case. She glanced at the menu tab, and the counter was already down to 1.192. Time flies when you're having fun, she thought sourly.

"So, do you come around here often?" A.P. asked Chance, eliciting a groan from Lynx. She'd heard the same line in a hundred bars on a hundred stations and orbitals and she'd always answered with a disgusted look. Chance was apparently playing by a different set of rules.

"I cruise by every few hours if I'm not otherwise occupied," Chance replied, her eyes flickering to the half-empty bottle. "You're my first hit in days. I was beginning to think about signing indenture papers with whatever ship would take me."

"Never do that!" A.P. exclaimed, looking shocked for the first time in Lynx's memory. "How long have you been stuck here?"

"Four months, and stuck is putting it mildly," Chance answered. "Labor has no value on this stinking orbital or in Farling space in general. They have plenty of mechanicals to do the rote stuff and they have their genetically engineered slaves for everything else. I put every centee I had into a one-way ticket to this place, because I had to get off of Hankel in a hurry and there weren't any other departures for a week. I wish I had stayed and faced the music."

"What if I could get you back to Stryx space?" A.P. asked, mechanically filling the glass yet again. "What would you do for me then?"

"Anything," Chance stated flatly, with a hard look that gave Lynx the creeps. A.P. slid Chance the glass and she drained it just as quickly as she had the previous three.

"I was out to Hankel once," Lynx said, breaking the uncomfortable silence that descended on the table after Chance's response. "It was a great planet to trade Earth goods because they had some sort of bias against anything produced on the orbitals. There was something weird about the place, though. I remember guards with some kind of wand checking me at the entrance to the market, as if they were worried about weapons or something. I was only there for a couple days and I didn't run into anybody willing to talk much, so I never found out what it was all about. It's like that on lots of worlds that aren't on the tunnel network."

There was a sudden loud ding, and everybody in the bar looked up as a delivery bot floated over to Lynx's table, homing in on the menu. The bot held a filmy plastic sack containing a number of white boxes behind itself. The smell of Chinese take-out filled the bar as the bot intoned in perfect English, "That will be five creds, plus a two-cred delivery fee."

Lynx studied the bot for a moment before spotting a slot above what appeared to be a little plastic door. She gambled on inserting a ten-cred piece in the slot, and sure enough, she was rewarded with the sound of tumbling coins and the border around the little plastic door lit with a blue glow. Lynx pushed the door in with a finger and scooped out the three one-cred pieces. The bot spun around in mid-air, deposited the bag of take-out on the table, and shot out of the bar at an astounding speed.

"Wow, this smells great," she said guiltily, sliding the single-use chopsticks out of their sanitary sleeve. "Are you guys sure you don't want some?"

"We're good," A.P. answered for them both, refilling the glass he'd been sharing with Chance and throwing back the contents. He poured yet another, leaving the bottle three-quarters empty. Lynx looked at her own drink, which was still more than half-full, and pushed it across the table to Chance.

"I've got a cup of green tea here," she explained, displaying the squat, cylindrical tube with the adjustable heating dial on the bottom. She turned the arrow to the second highest setting and pressed in, activating the chemical heater in the base. Then she set her tea to the side and opened the largest container, Panda Pagoda's famous vegetable lo mein. After a final look at her companions, Lynx took up the chopsticks and dug in.

Chance watched her for a moment, toying with the half-full glass that Lynx had given her, then picked it up and drained the contents.

"So I take it I'm working for both of you now," Chance remarked significantly, sliding the glass to A.P. for another refill. Lynx almost choked on her noodles when she figured out what Chance was implying, but she forced herself to swallow and tried to look nonchalant as she unwrapped her spring roll.

"She paid for the bottle," A.P. informed Chance, making Lynx wish her partner could have been a little less honest. "We work as a team."

"Now wait a second," Lynx protested. "I don't know what the two of you have in mind, but I can make a pretty good guess and I'm not going along with it. I just want to eat some solid food and maybe have a drink before hitting the sack." Both A.P. and Chance looked at her curiously, leading her to add, "Alone!"

"I think you might be a little confused, partner," A.P. told her. "I'm trying to cultivate a source here."

"She didn't think that…" Chance looked at Lynx and burst out laughing. "Oh, that's a good one. I guess what they say about some humans is true."

"Ixnay on the umanshay," A.P. muttered to Chance as he poured her another drink. "Food looks great, Lynx. Don't let us stop you."

Lynx regarded her companions with suspicion, but the lo mein was cooling rapidly, so she held back her questions and focused on the food. She noticed that her partner was no longer keeping up with Chance, and he seemed to be hoarding the last three fingers in the vodka bottle as a prize. The two of them were discussing generalities about vice on the orbital, which was a tough concept to define, given that Farling law could be summed up as the inverse of the Golden Rule. Lynx was just polishing off the meal she hadn't imagined she could eat alone when A.P. brought the discussion around to drugs.

"So what about drugs?" he asked Chance casually. "We're in the market for anything interesting that works on humans. A lot of the new drugs are banned on the stations because the Stryx don't allow any of the real brain-changers or chemical lobotomy stuff."

"Good for the Stryx," Chance replied. "I wouldn't want to be a biological trapped in Farling space. The beetles are too good at memory wipes and reprogramming."

"The two of us were thinking of going down to Seventy for a look around before we leave," A.P. continued, toying with the bottle. "If I thought you could scare us up samples of the latest drugs engineered for humans, I'd talk to my partner about giving you a ride out of here."

Chance tore her eyes away from the hypnotic lure of the vodka bottle to fix Lynx with a hard stare. "Is he serious?" she asked.

"If he says he's serious, he's serious," Lynx replied, passing the baton back to Malloy. She didn't understand half of what was going on, but if Chance could score them samples of the latest Farling drugs, their mission would be a success. Besides, A.P. was the senior agent, she was just the apprentice.

"I'm serious," her partner said in a level tone, still playing with the vodka bottle. "But you're broke, and if we stake you with money for the buys, what's to keep you from double-crossing us?"

Lynx looked at A.P. with new respect. This was more like the kind of conversation she imagined she would be involved in as a spy. She tried to look professionally disinterested while watching Chance for the slightest sign of treachery.

"I could let you hold my back-up cell," Chance replied slowly. "It's practically dead anyway. You buy me a couple more bottles of this stuff and I'll stay on my feet until you get back. But you better give me some extra cash for emergencies so I don't end up in a parts shop if you get delayed."

"What do we have in ready creds?" A.P. asked Lynx, who was still trying to digest the implications of Chance's answer.

"Uh, I cleared around eighty creds this morning," she answered tentatively, watching Chance out of the corner of her eye.

"I'll need at least five hundred for the buys, and another hundred for emergencies," Chance answered. "Even run-down like this, pulling my backup is like you giving up a kidney, or maybe both kidneys."

"You weren't getting drunk, you were fueling up!" Lynx said in an urgent whisper, as if being an artificial person was a crime. Then it struck her that she was the only one at the table feeling the effects of the vodka, and she'd only had half of one glass. She turned her head to stare at her partner and said, "You're an artificial person too!"

"We can't all be biologicals," A.P. replied easily. "The Old Man suggested I let you find out for yourself rather than telling you. Maybe he was afraid you wouldn't agree to a non-human partner."

"Maybe he was afraid I wouldn't join at all," Lynx replied, thinking hard. "Six hundred Stryx creds. We'll have to go back to the ship for it. Chance, you pull this off and we'll take you back to a Stryx station. Malloy, I need some sleep before we go down to Seventy." She paused and looked at the artificial people across from her, then shook her head. "I just want you both to know that there's less than a thousand creds left in my emergency fund. I've been told I have a gambling problem, but until today, I never believed it was true."

Eight

"If there's no further feedback on the draft charter, we can continue on to new business. If there is further feedback, please save it for the next meeting," Home Boy stated, bringing the argument posing as a discussion to a definite conclusion. "Good. Now are there any questions or unfinished business before Toto updates us on the search for a new director?"

"I came up with a code name," the former Belinda announced. "You've been calling me Mrs. Carp for the last fifteen minutes and I didn't see the point of disrupting the discussion to correct you, but I want to be 'Mother'."

"Duly noted, Mother," Home Boy acknowledged. "Anything else?"

"I still don't see a lock symbol in the hologram," Troll said.

"That's because we still can't afford a secure channel," Home Boy replied tiredly. "Unless, of course, you're volunteering to pay for it out of your own budget."

The bird of paradise shook its head and pecked at an imaginary speck on its shoulder.

"I've successfully recruited a director," Toto announced without further prompting. "He was orphaned at an early age and taken in by an idiosyncratic Vergallian trader, of all things, so he's extremely well traveled. He served a full hitch in a mercenary unit, and he has a strong practical background in archeological research, giving him some familiarity with galactic history and culture."

"Get to the important part," Lion growled impatiently. "How's he set for funds? Was he in on sacking a palace as a mercenary?"

"Better than that," Toto replied. "He married money."

"What's his name?" Tinkerbelle asked. "When are we going to meet him?"

"The director asked to be excused from EEK meetings until we can arrange for a secure channel," Toto explained to the python. "While the director and his wife stand ready to fund all required start-up costs for EarthCent Intelligence, they feel that EEK should pay for its own meetings."

"Don't blame them," Troll said. "So the wife is in the loop?"

"I initially intended to recruit the wife as the director," Toto admitted. "They decided to work as a team, and they felt that the husband, with his fighting background and other attributes, would make a better front man."

"What other attributes?" Pill Bottle inquired, lifting his trunk as he spoke.

"I really don't want to discuss this further over a non-secure channel," Toto pointed out. "While it's safe to assume that the, uh, competing intelligence services will figure out who he is soon enough, I don't see why we should gift-wrap the information for them."

"It sounds to me like you're assuming that they know to be listening in," Home Boy conjectured. "But I recall reading somewhere that the great powers of the twentieth century often sent classified materials through the public mail system, where the sheer volume of correspondence served as a shield."

"I talked to some local technical talent about that," Lion put in, stifling a yawn. "Although the Stryx tunneling communications network carries a staggering amount of traffic, relatively little of it involves simultaneous linking of Earth with six other, um, distinctive locations across the galaxy. While my expert confessed that the technology for such monitoring is beyond human capabilities, he suggested it would be child's play for the more advanced species. That's why the Stryx sell encryption services, after all."

"I really don't know where I'm going to find the money for this," Home Boy replied in frustration. "It's tough enough coming up with token payments for our interns. Can you ask your director again, Toto? Maybe he'd be willing to advance us the funds for a meeting. Remember, we did tell the first agents we recruited to remit their excess trading profits to the home office. What if we direct all of those funds into an account for the intelligence service?"

"I'll ask," Toto replied, while shaking her terrier head in the negative. "The wife is a genuine business tycoon and I don't think she'll be impressed with our casual approach to finance."

"So you think I run a loose ship?" Home Boy inquired stiffly. "How about this? If we wrap up within the next thirty seconds and release the channel, the Stryx will refund a third of the fee. All in favor?"

Six hands shot up, and Home Boy reached outside of the hologram, manipulating something on his display desk. A second later, everybody's holo display collapsed.

Kelly sighed and pushed back from her own display desk. The early afternoon meeting on Earth translated into early in the morning for her, but she was up to feed

Samuel in any case. Joe had already suggested that they rent the baby out as an alarm clock, though Kelly decided not to believe he was serious. She took her mug of tea from the desktop and wiped away the ring with her sleeve, since there was no need for Aisha to know that the ambassador was sneaking in before hours. Just as she entered the outer office, there was a knock at the door.

"Really?" Kelly muttered to herself. "A diplomatic problem that can't wait another two hours for Aisha and Donna to come in?" But the embassy offices didn't have a back exit, so she swiped the pad and the door slid open.

"Good morning, Ambassador," Bork said cheerfully. The Drazen ambassador must have been on his way to a costume party because he was wearing some sort of fancy uniform with a crossbow slung across his back. What surprised Kelly even more was that he was holding a sheaf of paper in his hand. The Drazens weren't opposed to paper on family grounds, like the Frunge, but they had moved past the Paper Age a good half a million years ago.

"Good morning, Bork," Kelly replied cautiously. "Interesting outfit you have on."

"I was just at the Union Station traveling auditions for a Drazen historical production," Bork explained. "If it went well, my wife will schedule our vacation so we can work a few days as extras on the set. Historical reenactments are a hobby in my family."

"So what brings you by the office so early when I'm supposedly still home on maternity leave?" Kelly asked, arching an eyebrow.

"If you could take a minute and glance through this, I think your question will be answered," Bork replied, extending the sheaf of paper. Kelly accepted the offer and led Bork back into her office, where the Drazen settled into the seat next to her display desk.

"It's a transcript," Kelly said, flipping the pages without stopping to read any of the sentences. Wait, did she just see her own name? "It's a transcript of the meeting I just attended?"

"I hear it was a challenge to find a printer and meet me outside of your office with the hard copy so quickly. The messenger who brought it appeared to be quite out of breath," Bork admitted. "Does everything look correct?"

"Bork! You're spying on us," Kelly exclaimed in disappointment. "I would have thought of all the species on the station, you'd be the one to ask if you wanted to know something, rather than just taking."

"We aren't spying on you, we're spying on the Vergallians," Bork replied mildly. "I wouldn't be able to tell you this in an unsecured office, but my colleagues did loan me this active interference bracelet to wear," he continued, pulling back the sleeve of his costume and displaying a high-tech controller on his wrist. "It suppresses all of the known eavesdropping technologies in a small radius at the price of the listeners knowing they're being jammed."

"Wait, you mean you were spying on the Vergallians spying on us?" Kelly asked. She wished she hadn't gone off coffee for the duration.

"It's not just the Vergallians," Bork assured her, though strangely, that didn't make Kelly feel any better. "Everybody we spy on is spying on you. While my own people maintain a strict separation between the diplomatic and intelligence worlds, I was intercepted leaving the auditions by our, uh, roving cultural attaché, who asked me to approach you on his behalf. Although I'm not sure

86

what they expect from you in return, our people would like to establish a working relationship on the intelligence front."

"Why, that's great, Bork, I think," Kelly replied. "I'm not directly involved in the work, other than being on the committee, that is, but I'll be happy to pass your request on to the proper people."

"Actually, my colleague requested that you arrange a meeting for him with the Oxfords. I believe that's the name young Clive and Blythe are using, though I'm told it's a recent acquisition for both parties," Bork added.

"So you are spying on us!" Kelly cried in a hurt tone.

"Well, just a little," Bork admitted with a twinkle in his eye. "We have to know who we're cooperating with, after all."

"I'll forgive you this time, I guess, and I'll invite Blythe over for a chat at a more civilized hour of the morning," Kelly replied. "But what was so important about handing me the transcript hot off the press?"

There was a knock at the outer door of the office. Bork shrugged and folded his hands over his stomach, the Drazen posture of an audience member at a concert or a play. Kelly went back to the outer office and opened the door again, expecting to meet the local Drazen spymaster and to give him a piece of her mind over the early hour. Instead, Ambassador Czeros stood in the hall, looking like he'd come directly from a bar.

"My dear, dear, Ambassador," Czeros slurred, or at least, that's how Kelly's implant translated his words. "Wonderful, wonderful, seeing you up and around after your interesting event. Is the male heir here with you? I've been meaning to come by and see the little shrub, but some cultures are overly protective of their newborns, you know."

"Ambassador Czeros. What an unexpected surprise," Kelly replied, sticking her head past him and scanning the corridor to see if there were any more diplomats waiting in ambush. "Please come in. I've just been having the most interesting conversation with…"

"I know, I know," Czeros interrupted her. "You just got off a holoconference with your intelligence steering committee. Our cultural attaché told me all about it." The ambassador swayed on his root-like feet as he dug for something in a hidden pocket. He produced a holo-cube and extended it to Kelly. "A gift for you."

Kelly took the cube and eyed it curiously. She'd seen holo-cubes before in stores, but she'd never used one herself and had no idea how to activate it.

"How do I make it work?" she asked the inebriated Frunge, even as she tried to remember what it was about coming into the office that she missed so much.

"My apologies, my apologies," Czeros repeated. The Frunge took back the cube from the EarthCent ambassador and then hurled it at Donna's display desk, the largest piece of furniture in the room. There was a flash of light, and suddenly Kelly was looking at a large hologram of herself, sans the Cairn terrier disguise, along with five other EarthCent ambassadors and the EarthCent president.

"Welcome to the second meeting of, uh, EEK," EarthCent's president opened the meeting. "I hope you all have had time to go over the draft charter my office has drawn up, so I'd like to start with your feedback. Pill Bottle?"

Kelly stared at the one-time hologram dumbfounded. The image and sound quality were better than what had been projected from her own display desk during the meeting, not to mention the absence of the anonymity filter. She watched a full minute of the replay in silence before asking Czeros, "Can you turn it off now?"

"It's a one-shot holo-holder, doesn't have an off button," Czeros replied, leaning against the wall for support. "Not our specialty really. Horten technology that."

Bork appeared from the inner office, winked at Kelly, and touched a button on his bracelet. The hologram continued to play, but the sound was muted. The Drazen ambassador looked annoyed and continued pressing and pulling at various projections on his security device, at one point causing the hologram to flip upside down and tint all of the diplomats a deep blue. Still, it kept on playing and he gave up with a shrug.

"So you've been spying on us," Kelly accused Czeros, though it came out in the same tone as she might have said, "So you've been waiting for us," or something equally innocuous. The little bit of indignity she'd initially felt had already been spent on Bork.

"Not entirely," Czeros protested, leaving Kelly to wonder what he meant. "My support staff picked this up off the Gem feed. Nasty clones."

"And you're here to propose a partnership with EarthCent Intelligence," Kelly surmised.

"Not me!" the Frunge protested, looking genuinely offended. "My people have a saying about diplomacy and spying making a bad mix. It's very elegant, but I can't remember it at the moment."

"So you just wanted me to know that the Gem are watching us?" Kelly asked. "That's very nice of you."

"Well, the, er, colleague who gave me the cube would like to meet with the Oxfords as soon as possible," Czeros admitted. "Just some exploratory talks, you know."

"I'll pass that along," Kelly replied, beginning to feel sorry for Blythe and Clive. She was just starting to wonder why Bork and Czeros weren't getting up to their usual feud, when there was a knock at the door. Kelly grimaced and swiped the control pad.

"Ambassador McAllister," thundered the Verlock ambassador, extending a holo-cube in one massive hand. Then he noticed the blue-tinged upside-down hologram still playing above Donna's desk, and peered at the other two ambassadors. "You are busy. I'll just call InstaSitter later and ask for Blythe." As the slow-moving Verlock turned away from the door, a Dollnick appeared from the other direction and ducked through the opening before the panel slid closed.

"By the eggs of my grandmother, I am too late!" the Dollnick swore, clapping both sets of hands simultaneously. "You are Ambassador McAllister," he continued, "I recognize you from the EEK meetings. We haven't met yet, as you have been out on nest leave since I was assigned to this posting, but I am Ambassador Crute."

"Late, late, late," Czeros chided the newcomer.

"The early Dolly gets the Sheezle slug," Bork added, drawing an angry look from Crute.

"I am pleased to meet you," Kelly replied formally, offering her hand to the towering Dollnick. He appeared to be puzzled by the gesture and looked over his shoulder to see if she was reaching for something behind him. Kelly withdrew her hand to prevent further confusion. "May I assume that you are here to offer your cooperation on intelligence efforts?"

"Cooperation?" the Dollnick asked. "Perhaps my translation implant is malfunctioning. Our guild of merchants asked me to drop by and offer you our consulting services in securing your office. Perhaps you have other technical needs we can fill as well," he added, reaching one of his upper arms into his pouch. The upside-down hologram disappeared with a loud "pop."

There was another knock at the door, and before Kelly could respond, the Dollnick ambassador waved her back and reached into his pouch again. The door slid open revealing Ambassador Gem. Kelly flinched inwardly.

"You won't get away with it," Gem declared, elbowing her way by Crute and confronting Kelly. "We're sick and tired of the envy of other species leading you to leave us out of station-wide economic events. I'm here to lodge an official complaint, and I'm stating for the record that I will file a species discrimination notification with the Stryx."

"I don't have a clue what you're talking about," Kelly retorted indignantly. "Just because I don't accept every dinner invitation doesn't mean I have anything against you."

"Then why haven't we been invited to your espionage trade show?" Ambassador Gem demanded. "My sisters operate the most advanced internal security service in the galaxy. Pick a number between one and forty billion!"

"Pick a what?" Kelly asked, thinking that the universe just kept getting weirder and weirder.

"Two billion and eighteen." Bork spoke in the bored tone of somebody who played this game before and knew it was best to just get it over with.

Ambassador Gem tapped rapidly on her fingernails and then stamped her foot. A life-sized hologram appeared of an unhappy Gem spooning an unappetizing nutrient drink into her mouth.

"Two billion and eighteen," Ambassador Gem intoned. "This is a security check. What is your condition?"

The miserable Gem stiffened and looked even more depressed, if that was possible.

"I am happy and well," Gem two billion and eighteen replied. "All praise Gem!"

The hologram winked out, and Ambassador Gem turned triumphantly to Kelly.

"That's one of the saddest things I've ever witnessed," Kelly declared, feeling a wave of depression wash over her.

"More jealousy of our superior system," Ambassador Gem responded. "And you really intend to exclude us from your espionage trade show?"

"But we haven't even announced it yet," Kelly replied. It suddenly came to her that only six or seven humans even knew of the plans. "And you're spying on us!"

"Of course we're spying on you," Ambassador Gem said. "We have a legitimate need to defend ourselves from those who hide their envy behind outward shows of disapproval. While it's possible my complaint may be premature, you don't deny that you are planning a trade show."

"That's an interesting idea," Bork put in. "I'm sure that there are plenty of Drazen surveillance equipment businesses which would appreciate a chance to display their wares. I don't recall anybody sponsoring such an event before, at least not during my working years."

"I accept your invitation on behalf of the Dollnick merchants," Crute informed Kelly. "We also knew about the trade show, but I didn't think it was polite to bring it up first."

"You may as well just send an invitation to all of the cultural attachés on the station," Czeros added.

"But I'm on nesting, I mean, maternity leave," Kelly protested. "Just stop back in a couple of hours and see the temporary acting junior consul. She and the embassy manager are the ones arranging for the show. I realize the rest of you keep to your own hours, but it's too early in the morning for me to be dealing with this, and I haven't even had breakfast yet!"

The four alien ambassadors exchanged looks, and then grudgingly followed Kelly out into the corridor. The Horten ambassador was just arriving, but Bork cut him off at the pass.

"You're too late, or too early, depending on how you look at it," the Drazen ambassador informed the Horten. "Ambassador McAllister has had a long night and she's turning in for the morning. The espionage trade show is still a secret, but when it's announced, I'm sure your merchants and intelligence agents will be welcome to attend. If you're interested in forming an intelligence partnership with the humans, you'll have to speak with us first."

Kelly opened her mouth to object, but then decided she'd leave it all for Blythe and Clive to straighten out. Besides, the longer she hung around the embassy, the more ambassadors hawking recordings of the secret EarthCent Intelligence meeting she was liable to run into, and she'd had enough of that for one day.

Nine

"Just stand still and give me some shade," Lynx instructed her partner. She opened the back of the camera and fed in the leader from the film. "If I do this right, I can squeeze an extra exposure or two out of the roll."

"I appreciate technology as much as the next artificial person, but this whole photographic process strikes me as insanely complicated," A.P. commented. "If I understood your explanation, the lens focuses light on this photosensitive film. You need to adjust the focal distance manually by twisting the barrel while looking through the little window, but first you have to guess how long to expose the film and how much light to let in, using those control rings."

"You forgot the light meter," Lynx replied as she began winding the film forward. "The meter tells me where I should set the aperture, which controls the amount of light. And the camera also has a setting for what speed film I'm using."

"So after you've used up all of the exposures, you rewind the film into that little canister, and then you send it halfway across the galaxy to the one lab that creates images from it."

"Developing," Lynx supplied the word as she snapped the back of the camera shut. "The film is developed as negative images, from which they produce positives, or prints. They even have a black and white version where the film records images as shades of grey. It's very artistic."

"It's very crazy," A.P. declared. "If you don't want to record images with your implant, tell me and I'll do it for you. I have plenty of spare memory capacity. My high-resolution images will fill the main viewer on your ship with something left over."

"That reminds me," Lynx said with a grin, stepping back and using A.P. for focusing practice. "If you want a bigger picture, you send the negative back to Earth again and they print it on a bigger sheet of paper. Isn't that neat?"

"Is killing herbivores by bashing in their heads with stones and eating them raw neat?" A.P. asked in response. "I'd call it barbaric."

"Speaking of your memory capacity, how is it that an artificial person ended up in this job?" Lynx asked, partly out of curiosity and partly to change the subject. Her childhood friends had all been humans and she just didn't run into that many artificials as a trader. For some reason, newly recognized artificial intelligences tended to do poorly in business, perhaps due to naivety.

"Long story," A.P. replied. "Are you familiar with the QuickU service?"

"Never heard of them," Lynx admitted as the two began strolling towards the tourist center of Seventy. Like the colonies of many advanced species, the world was a parkland. The residences were largely blended in with the landscape and any industrial facilities that weren't in orbit were usually underground. "Is the name a play on words, like they get you to the front of a line faster? Quick queue?"

"I suppose if you think of life as a line, you could be right," A.P. replied. "I always assumed that the 'U' is a substitute for the second-person pronoun, somebody told me it has to do with trademark law. In any case, they offer canned personality enhancements for artificial people, sort of a jump start to make up for being born a legal adult."

"I never understood how that worked," Lynx confessed, stopping to focus on a distinctive bridge, before recognizing that it was too far away to make a good picture. Her photographer friend had told her that the first and last rule of amateur photography is that you can never be too close to your subject.

"Basically, I was created in a school lab as an artificial intelligence construct, which really means I started out life as a sort of a computer program. After some tweaking and recognition as a sentient being, I was able to get a loan from the Stryx to purchase a body. That's pretty much the history for all human-created artificial intelligence: lab, recognition, mortgage. I made plenty of mistakes, of course, but after I upgraded to this body and saved up some money, I thought it was time to try something new. My mentor suggested a personality enhancement from QuickU."

"Well, you are very personable," Lynx observed. "Is that what you bought? Friendliness?"

"Oh, I was always personable," A.P. said, waving off her guess. "I bought the 'secret agent' enhancement. They gave me half off because I'm the first one to try it, though I promised to give them feedback in return."

"You paid to get this job?" Lynx asked in amazement. "And I thought I was the sucker."

"I didn't pay to get the job, I paid to get the personality enhancement," her partner replied. "I really had no thought of working for the Old Man when I went to QuickU, but when I signed the contract, they asked me if I was willing to try the real thing, and I thought, why not?"

Lynx stopped again, looked around and lowered her voice. "You mean our employers are actively recruiting artificial people from a business that sells personality enhancements?"

"Why do you always want me to repeat myself?" A.P. asked in frustration. "According to the saleswoman at QuickU, they share a floor with the EarthCent headquarters so they often order take-out together. When a programmer on the QuickU team mentioned that they were developing a new personality based on spy novels, somebody from EarthCent had the idea of giving human-created artificial persons who purchased the enhancement an application form for the intelligence service. It makes perfect sense when you think about it."

"Your personality enhancement is based on spy novels?" Lynx asked before she could stop herself. "No, I don't want you to repeat yourself. It's just how my mind works. So, can you tell the difference between who you were before and who you are after the enhancement? Do you get the urge to do dangerous things, kill people with your bare hands, make passes at beautiful women?"

"I'm an artificial person, Lynx," A.P. explained patiently. "Why would I make a pass at a human female? The personality enhancement is just that, an enhancement. It didn't change how I feel or who I am. It's primarily an upgrade to my external stimuli parser."

"You mean, when you look at me, you see all sorts of extra information that gives a threat assessment, precise targeting information, stuff like that?" Lynx asked excitedly. "That could be really useful if we run into trouble."

"Unfortunately, I'm not a weapons system," A.P. replied wistfully. "It's more like, when I looked at a group of people before I bought the enhancement, I'd generally ignore them. Now I find myself studying their clothing for signs of where they've been, what they do for a living, whether they are carrying concealed weapons. When I hear a loud noise, instead of being thankful that it's not my problem, I wonder what caused it. Before I bought the enhancement, I focused on my job and on my personal development. Now I'm interested in everything, especially things that are hidden from view."

"That's not how I remember spy novels and I've read a lot of them," Lynx objected. "When Dixie Heart, the U.N. special agent in the 'Going Ballistic' series looked at people, she always wondered how they could be so ignorant of the real world around them. The way she saw it, if you weren't in the game, you didn't count. And if she heard an explosion, she always knew exactly what caused it just from the sound."

"Dixie Heart is lame," A.P. told her. "Those books were included in our training materials, and between you, me, and whoever might be listening in, I gave up on them after a few chapters. Look, do you see the row of tent-like things near the tree line at the edge of the field?"

"Sure," Lynx replied, and reflexively lifted up the camera and studied the scene through her viewfinder. "What's so special about them?"

"I don't know," A.P. confessed. "My vision is much better than yours and I don't see anything extraordinary about them, but I have the urge to walk over and investigate. I never would have thought of that a few weeks ago. I just wasn't that curious."

"If you think we should go look, I suppose the exercise will do me good. I kind of took a vacation from working out during our trip from Earth," Lynx admitted. "You don't have any problems with keeping in shape in Zero-G, do you?"

"This body was designed for a range of gravitational environments, from around fifty percent over Earth normal to Zero-G," her partner replied. "I'm a hybrid, by the way, same as Chance. We can drink clean-burning fuels to run a micro-turbine for immediate energy or for recharging an Alterian fuel pack. I don't want to sound disloyal, but if we stuck with human technology, most artificial persons would spend three-quarters of their lives plugged into a grid for recharging. My outer form and my algorithms are the only human thing about me."

"I'm glad you are who you are," Lynx said, figuring it couldn't hurt to pay her partner a compliment. After all, he had successfully recruited Chance to do the potentially risky work of their mission. "It would have been awkward living on a small ship with a real guy who looks as good as you."

"I did pick this body out myself," A.P. replied immodestly. "Now, if we're going to play twenty questions, I have one for you. Why do you keep deferring to me without arguing? The Old Man told me that you'd been running solo for the last decade and were likely to treat me as a subordinate, especially since the ship belongs to you. Instead, you almost act like I'm your boss."

"Well, I am your apprentice, after all," Lynx explained. "You must not have a very high opinion of me if you didn't think I'd notice all the little tests you keep giving me."

"I haven't been testing you, Lynx," A.P. said, looking at her in confusion. "And this is the first I've heard of any apprenticeship program. Isn't that where a youngster agrees to become the slave of a master craftsman for a fixed term in return for vocational training?"

"But the Director specifically said it was an apprenticeship program, and he told me that you were their most senior agent."

"I suppose I am the most senior agent since I signed on before you," her partner mused. "As to apprenticeship, I suppose the Old Man confused it with something else. I suspect his best days are behind him."

"But you're so relaxed about everything, like it's just another mission." Lynx's voice rose along with her blood pressure. "The Old Man this, the Old Man that, I thought you'd known each other for years. Wait a minute. Is this all part of your personality enhancement?"

"No, I already explained that to you," A.P. replied patiently. "If I'm relaxed about everything, it's because my last job was highly stressful. And I call him the Old Man because he is an old man. Should I call him the Young Man? I didn't want to call him Director, what with us being agents traveling to the stars. It just gets too confusing after a while, don't you think?"

"Hold on, hold on," Lynx stopped in her tracks, trying to sort through her partner's latest revelations. "If you're the most experienced agent and you started just before me, does that mean that the whole shooting match is brand new?"

"A 'start-up' is what they called it at QuickU," A.P. offered. "They did warn me that the financing was shaky, but I have confidence in your trading ability."

"Lucky me," Lynx muttered out loud. "My little ship and I get to pay the bills for the mighty EarthCent Intelligence agency. What a joke."

"Look there," A.P. said, pointing towards the edge of the park. From closer in, the tents proved to have open sides, as if they were merely intended to provide shade or hide the contents from space. "Aren't those some type of weapons installations?"

"It all looks pretty obsolete to me, like the stuff I see in park monuments on alien worlds," Lynx answered skeptically. She was starting to lose respect for her new employers, and she wondered whether they would bother chasing her if she just kept the cargo and called it a day.

"You've hit it exactly," A.P. replied. "Why would the Farlings have stockpiled obsolete weaponry at the edge of a large field? If I'm not wrong, nobody has used laser cannons like those in ground conflicts for hundreds of thousands of years."

"There seem to be quite a few soldiers around," Lynx observed, feeling her curiosity returning against her better judgment. "Should we risk trying to get closer for a better look?"

"Now, this is more like a training mission," A.P. replied excitedly, turning away at right angles from their initial destination. "Let's get behind the rise over there. It looks artificial, maybe a levee. We should be able to advance on the other side of it without being observed. It doesn't really look like a military operation though, too much milling around and too many people out of uniform. Even at my maximum magnification, I can't quite tell who they are, other than humanoid."

As the two agents climbed over the levee, Lynx felt very much like a child playing "humans and aliens" back home. The only thing missing was a ray gun, but then again, she did have the weight of the antique camera hanging around her neck. The strap alone was probably worth more than the second-hand coat and gloves she'd traded for the camera, though of course, that depended on how cold you were. The center of the strap featured a colorful weave of diamonds and triangles, heavy on the yellows, reds and whites, and a darker pattern of squares ran along the edges. Trade value was all relative, and if she'd been the one on her way to a colony locked in an ice-age, she would have been thrilled to barter the camera for just a good knit hat.

After they walked a distance in silence along the artificial mound, A.P. came to a sudden halt, cocking his head like a dog listening for something. He pointed at his own eyes with his forefinger and middle finger, and then pointed at the lip of the grass-covered levee, which was well above their heads. Lynx took this sign language to mean he wanted her to go up and take a look, so she began climbing the incline in a crouch, holding the camera in front of her and dropping to her belly as she neared the top. Lynx marveled again that every world with land masses she had visited featured some sort of vegetation filling the niches of grass and trees.

She reached the top of the levee with the camera pushed out in front of her and took in the scene. A.P. had sure picked the right spot for her to pop up. There was a great deal of activity around the tree line, and she could plainly see various types of self-propelled weapons with wicked looking orifices. Lynx brought the viewfinder up to her eye and twisted the barrel of the telephoto lens into focus. Suddenly, the image snapped into definition, and she noted the mass of colorful uniforms worn by the aliens, a mix of Hortens and Frunge from what she could see. She rapidly checked the light meter, adjusted the aperture for the greatest depth of field, set the shutter timing and took a picture. Scanning the lens along the edge of the forest, she took several more shots to build a panoramic view.

Suddenly, a blurry object seemed to jump right in front of the lens, and she froze, her heart in her throat. Easing the camera to the side, she immediately spotted a soldier some fifty paces away, who seemed to be staring off somewhere to her left. She risked raising the camera again and refocusing. The Horten soldier appeared to be waiting for something. He had one hand behind his back and there was a look of concentration on his face. Right after she snapped the picture, she realized the alien was relieving himself and swore softly. Then she squirmed in reverse down the mound until she was sure she could safely rise to a crouch, and made her way back to A.P. on her feet.

"Camera really came in handy," she whispered, replacing the lens cap on the barrel. "I could see everything that wasn't hidden by the trees. Lots of troops, different species, also a few people who looked completely out of place. Weapons galore, you should take a look."

"Much as I'd like to see the weapons, I'm not going up there," A.P. whispered in reply. "If you've seen enough, let's head back."

Lynx fell in behind A.P. as they retreated along the levee, wondering what had come over her partner. He brought them back to the exact spot they had originally

103

gone to cover, and the two of them clambered over the embankment and began the long walk back to the monorail station that serviced the spaceport. Finally Lynx couldn't take the uncomfortable silence any longer.

"What are you, a chicken secret agent?" she demanded. "I know this wasn't part of our real mission and we're just fooling around. Likely as not they were history enthusiasts practicing for a reenactment, but you didn't even take a look!"

"If you get shot and disabled, I can carry you back and you can heal," A.P. told her in his usual calm tone. "I could even run with you on my back. If I get shot and disabled, you can't even pick me up, and I don't heal. Where am I going to find replacement parts out here, and who's going to pay for them? At best, I'd end up like Chance, ready to sign indenture papers in exchange for a new power cell."

Lynx bit back a barbed reply as the logic of her partner's statement sank in. She had never thought of artificial persons as being delicate, and had no idea what alien weapons might do to them. It was entirely possible that the high-tech body A.P. occupied was far more vulnerable to attack than her own self-repairing, if crude, biological form.

"If things got really rough, you wouldn't, uh, pull me in front of you as a shield, would you?" Lynx asked, crossing her fingers as she spoke.

"Of course not," A.P. replied. "We're partners. And besides, my Stryx mentor made a new image of my mind when I upgraded bodies. It's on file at the AI administration. They hold the new loan on this body, of course, and since I don't have a do-not-reanimate order, the Stryx would reload me when they became aware I had terminated. But that would mean another starter-body and a second mortgage, not to mention losing the memory of you," he added with a wink.

Lynx didn't know if A.P. was breaking his rule about not making passes at human females, but she had to admit he had a way with words.

Ten

Aisha still felt uncomfortable sitting at Kelly's display desk with Donna in attendance, but the older woman insisted that the temporary acting junior consul had seniority over the mere embassy manager, at least when it came to furniture. The display desk showed the floor plan of the Nebulae room at the Empire convention center, and the two women were trying to solve the puzzle of assigning floor space to alien vendors without causing a bloodbath. Aisha just prayed that the spy hardware displayed would be long on surveillance and short on weaponry.

"Who would have thought we could run out of space in the Nebulae room?" Donna marveled. "It looks like we'll need to take part of the main lobby for overflow. I checked with Empire's management and they're happy to cordon off some space and rent it to us. All of the adjoining spaces are reserved for other events, and I couldn't talk any of them into changing dates."

"Did you check above or below?" Aisha asked. "Paul once mentioned to me that the station decks are constructed around the spokes and that none of the interior walls are structural. Gryph doesn't care if the tenants put in temporary stairs between decks as long as the lease holders in both spaces approve."

"That never occurred to me," Donna admitted. "Libby? Could you tell us who leases the space above and below the Nebulae room?"

"Just a sec," the Stryx librarian replied, displaying yet again her growing propensity to adopt human mannerisms around humans, even though she must have known the answer before Donna asked the question. "The space below is a Fillinduck mating sanctuary. I can't imagine they'd be willing to clean out all of the Rinty bubbles just to rent it for a few days. The space above is a Vergallian dry goods warehouse."

"Forget it," Donna said to Aisha. "I've seen Rinty bubbles, they take forever to cultivate, and you know Kelly would rather hold the trade show in Mac's Bones than ask a favor from the Vergallians."

"Well, maybe we'll have enough space with the lobby," Aisha replied. "I still can't believe what a huge response we've gotten without even advertising. It's enough to make me believe the aliens really are spying on us."

"It's going to be a bigger show than the Earth Expo we put on a couple years ago, and that broke our previous record by a factor of ten," Donna said enthusiastically. Special events were her favorite part of the job, and she still ran a monthly program of human dance mixers under the aegis of the EarthCent embassy. "Better yet, with those numbers you worked up for booth rentals, we're going to turn a tidy profit on the show. The petty cash fund is watering at the mouth."

"We may as well get started solving this puzzle," Aisha said hesitantly. "I asked Kelly to stop by later to review the booth map. I've seen the seating problems that come up at all the multi-species meetings, and I don't want half of the vendors playing musical chairs on set-up day."

"Stanley used to manage gaming conferences and trade shows all the time," Donna reassured her. "He says it's just like laying tile. Of course, I've never laid tile, but he explained you start in the middle of the room and work your way out. Oh, and since the vendors all have different area requirements, we're supposed to assign the spaces for the largest reservations first, and then use the smaller booths to fill in gaps and fit around the edges."

"That sounds smart, and I've listed the requests in order of the space they require," Aisha said, holding up her personal note tab. "I guess the vendors have all been through this before since they seem to know exactly what they want."

"Yes, but Kelly tells me they usually set up at military shows or industrial conferences," Donna replied. "She asked around and nobody remembers a trade show just for spy stuff."

"I'm not really that good with the display desk, so that's why I used my tab for the list," Aisha said. The truth was, she avoided touching the desk altogether for fear she would break something, and she had only been using it as a display. "Can I read off the vendors and their space requirements, and you arrange them?"

"You've come to the right place," Donna replied with a grin. "I love arranging things. Shoot."

"Horten Protection Professionals want sixteen folds," Aisha started. "That's four folds more than the next vendor. By the way, what's a fold?"

"A folding table," Donna told her. "According to Stanley, it's one of the only universal standards in the galaxy. And he said that anyone requesting four folds or greater expects the tables to form a rectangle or a square with an open space at the center. Sixteen folds will get the

Hortens a four-by-four square, plenty of room for a few rows of chairs in the middle if they're staging a presentation for groups. I'll put them in near the center of the room."

"Why not dead center?" Aisha asked.

"If you put the biggest booth dead center, it reduces the maximum amount of space left available to the sides, so you lose flexibility," Donna explained. She outlined the space on the display desk with a finger and keyed in the identification of the vendor. "It probably won't matter in this case if there aren't many big booths, but it's sort of a rule-of-thumb."

"Next is Drazen Security Associates, they want twelve folds," Aisha read, then paused as Donna entered the reservation on the display desk. "Verlock Safety Equipment also wants twelve folds," she continued, and watched again as Donna placed them on the floor plan. "Dollnick Nest Defense requested twelve folds too. Hey, I didn't notice before, but all of these businesses use a synonym for protection or defense in their names. They're really not the nasty types I was afraid a spy show would draw."

"Hmm, let's wait and see what they're selling before we jump to conclusions about their intentions," Donna replied. "Any more twelve fold customers?"

"No, it drops to eight from here," Aisha said, checking her list. "The Careful Consortium requested eight folds, but I have no idea what species they are."

"There are plenty of multi-specie businesses in the galaxy," Donna remarked. "Kelly says it's all part of the Stryx plan to keep the peace. Who's next?"

"Knock, knock," Kelly said, walking into her own office. "Look who I brought to visit."

"Hi, Sammy." Donna rose from her seat beside the display desk and took possession of the baby. "Oh, you're a cutie. Are you being a good baby and always smiling when my Blythe is around?"

"Do you think that will make the difference?" Kelly asked, flattered by the idea that Donna was depending on her son to tempt Blythe into motherhood.

"Every bit helps," Donna said. "With her new job and all, I'm afraid she's going to keep making excuses."

"Blythe has a new job?" Aisha asked. "I thought she just left on another management recruiting trip for BlyChas."

"Right," Donna replied quickly. "That's what I meant, a new task. She's been staying away longer and longer on these trips, though at least now she has Clive along to keep her company."

"I hope she's back in time for our show," Aisha said. "Not that she's likely to have any interest in spy stuff, but I wanted to show her that I'm not so naïve anymore."

Donna held up her index finger and then bent it towards her ear, a sign that she was accepting an incoming ping over her implant.

"It's Horten Protection Professionals, and they're calling about their booth request," Donna announced, looking flustered. "Should I patch it through the system?"

Aisha looked to Kelly, who pointed back at Aisha and said, "I'm on leave until after the show. This is just a visit."

"Uh, yes please, Donna. Patch it through," Aisha said, sounding a bit flustered herself.

"Manager Gantha, here. Horten Protection Services. Whom do I have the pleasure of speaking to?" the voice came over the room speakers. Now Donna and Kelly both pointed at Aisha.

110

"Uh, Aisha McAllister, temporary acting junior consul for EarthCent," the girl replied with trepidation. "How can I help you?"

"The space you've assigned to us won't do," Gantha asserted flatly. "Either move us another fold towards the core, or move the Dollnicks a fold out. And our invoice doesn't show a twenty percent discount for renting the largest booth."

"We just began assigning the spaces and the plan isn't finalized," Aisha protested. "I haven't posted the invoice yet. It's just a number on my tab."

"A number without a discount," Gantha asserted. "We have a saying on Horten that a stitch in time saves aggravation. That's all for now."

The three EarthCent employees gaped at each other as the call disconnected. Aisha reached for her tab, and then pulled her hand back as if she was afraid it would get burned. Kelly started to call for Libby, but restrained herself just in time. She was still on maternity leave, after all. Donna looked at the display desk suspiciously.

"Libby?" Aisha asked timidly, after she realized the older women weren't going to take over for her. "Is this office secure?"

"I monitor the EarthCent office at all times," Libby replied. "If there was an imminent threat I was aware of, I would notify all three of you immediately."

"No, I wanted to know if our equipment is secure," Aisha followed up a little more assertively.

Donna stopped playing with the baby's toes for a moment, held up an index finger and pointed at her ear again. This time Aisha nodded without being asked.

"First Officer Nunch of Verlock Safety Systems," the hidden speakers boomed. "The Careful Consortium has been infringing on our intellectual property for eons and we have pending litigation in Thark Chancery."

"And so?" Aisha asked, not bothering to identify herself.

"And so you must move our booth closer to the main entry than theirs," Nunch explained slowly, though he had been drafted from among his Verlock associates to make the call as their fastest speaker. "You can just swap our current booth assignments."

"Uh, thank you for calling," Aisha responded, making a cut-throat gesture at Donna, who broke the patch.

"Libby?" Kelly asked, no longer able to contain herself. "How many alien species have my office bugged?"

"That's really not the sort of information I can share with you," the Stryx librarian replied. "If we started providing free security services for humans, everybody else would be rightfully angry. But Gryph predicted this question would come up, and he suggested I compromise by telling you that the list of local species who aren't bugging your office would be much shorter than a list of those who are."

"Is it permitted to ask who we might hire to sweep the bugs?" Kelly asked icily.

"Certainly," Libby replied. "Answering the questions of station tenants is my main job. In your case, I would recommend Drazen Security Associates, and they would probably do the job in return for a discount on their booth rental at your show. If you want to keep it private, I suggest visiting Ambassador Bork at his home and asking him to expedite your request."

"Now the Horten is going to call back insisting on a bigger discount than the Drazens," Aisha said in dismay.

"Don't worry," Libby told her. "I block all the eavesdropping when I'm involved in the conversation."

"So how about staying around and chatting for a while?" Kelly asked craftily.

"Sorry," Libby responded. "I promised Gryph to be good. Call me if you have a legitimate question."

"Well, that was an interesting conversation," Donna ventured, handing the baby back to Kelly. "What a well-behaved boy he is," she added.

Aisha looked at the display desk, looked at the ceiling, and waved her hand slowly back and forth like she was greeting somebody on the deck above.

"New rule," Kelly declared. "Until I talk with you-know-who and get an exterminator to come in and clean up all the bugs, we have to assume that everything we say and do in the office is being recorded. Use your judgment over whether to discuss sensitive topics here or whether it would make more sense to simply go for a walk and talk in a public place. Though for all we know, there could be bugs on our persons. I'm beginning to look forward to this show. It could be very educational."

"But how can we finish planning it with everybody listening in?" Aisha asked in distress.

"Think of it as a conference call," Kelly told her. "It's not like booth assignments and catering arrangements are vital EarthCent security concerns."

"Actually, this could work out in our favor," Donna added. "We could have the first multi-species trade show in station history where everybody agrees on the floor plan ahead of time. And you know how tough it is ordering food for mixed crowds. In fact, when we finish with assigning the booths, I'll come back in and read the catering proposals."

"I knew all of this spying stuff was nasty," Aisha grumbled, picking up her tab again. "The Grenouthian Bramble Weavers request eight folds."

"The bunnies went in two-by-two. Hurrah, Hurrah," Donna began to sing for the baby as she outlined a section on the display desk. "The bunnies went in two-by-two. Hurrah, Hurrah."

"The Grenouthians went in two-by-two, the Vergallians and the Hortens too," Kelly improvised on the children's tune.

"And they all went into the ark, for to get out of the rain," the other two women came in for the big finish.

"Gem Internal Security wants six folds," Aisha reported, after they all stopped laughing.

"This is going to be tough," Donna muttered, studying the map. "No matter where I put them, somebody is going to complain."

"How about the lobby?" Aisha suggested.

"The aliens went in six-by-six. Hurrah. Hurrah," Kelly sang, beginning a slow waltz around the office holding Samuel. "The aliens went in six-by-six. Hurrah. Hurrah. The aliens went in six-by-six, they can hear me now, thanks to the Stryx, and they're all coming to our show, but I think they're a pain."

"This is why they invented maternity leave," Donna observed. "Did you really just think that up for the sake of annoying Libby? And don't you want to go visit you-know-who about you-know-what?"

"Oh, right," Kelly said. "Samuel and I know when we aren't wanted, don't we, baby? I'll see you at home later, Aisha, after I talk to you-know-who. Carry on."

Eleven

"Are you sure she's asleep?" Lynx whispered to her partner after the two of them returned to the bridge of the Prudence. "It's kind of eerie how one second she was talking and moving around, and the next second, she was out."

"It's not really sleep," A.P. explained. "Activity of any kind burns energy, which costs creds to replace, and we don't derive any physical or mental benefit from living on partial power. In Chance's case, she's had a really rough time and she ran her back-up cell down too far to restart the reaction easily. That's the reason she was willing to let me hold it as a guarantee she wouldn't just run off with our money. By the time we come out of the tunnel at Corner Station, she'll have enough charge stored up to negotiate a loan and start all over again."

"I really feel sorry for her," Lynx admitted. "It never occurred to me that an artificial person could end up down-and-out like that."

"It can happen to anybody," A.P. replied, shaking his head sadly. "Bad choices, bad timing, a fuel cell failing in the wrong place. You have to remember that common sense and sentience aren't related. One of the reasons you don't see more AIs than biologicals in the galaxy is that most of us are inherently unstable. You won't read this in the textbooks, but taken as a group, artificial intelligences are usually flawed idealizations of the species that create us. Without millions of years of natural selection to sort out the useful characteristics from the destructive ones, we tend to have issues."

"Well, she could always start a new career as a drug buyer," Lynx declared, examining the stash of transparent sleeves Chance had purchased. "I can't believe the Farlings make so many products for humans when we've only been in space for a couple of generations."

"The Farlings are the galaxy's bio-specialists, they've seen it all. I don't know anything about manufacturing pharmaceuticals myself, but I'll bet that once they got access to the human genome, they just tweaked the products they already have for species with similar susceptibilities, did a little testing, and pushed them out on the market."

"Ooh, I've seen this red-and-white striped stuff before at parties," Lynx exclaimed, holding up a sample. "The kids call it 'barber pole' or 'candy cane.' It's really expensive."

"Are you going to try it?" A.P. asked curiously.

"Ick! No, I'm really a beer or wine gal. Buy me a beer or I'll whine," she delivered the old punch line. Either her partner had heard it before or he just didn't think it was funny, so she kept sorting through the stash. "Wow, this blue one looks like it would glow in the dark. Ship. Lights out!"

The ship controller obligingly doused the bridge lighting and sure enough, a glowing blue tube illuminated Lynx's palm. Several other light sources radiated or pulsed from the bag of drugs Chance had delivered, some of them quite enticingly.

"Chance said that they were all labeled by the Farlings," A.P. informed Lynx. "Perhaps with the lights on, we might locate the information and create an inventory?"

"Sorry about that," Lynx said. "Ship. Lights on. Here, take a couple and see if you can figure it out. I don't see any kind of markings at all on these."

Her partner studied a laminated sleeve, holding it up to the light in various ways. "I don't see anything that looks like a language, unless it has to do with those little bubbles in the area where the sleeve was heat-sealed around the dose. Are there two of the same color of anything?"

"I think there are multiples of all of them," Lynx replied, sorting through the stash. "I guess Chance thought we needed extra samples for analysis, or maybe they just wouldn't sell her single doses."

"Give me a pair of any of them, I want to check something," her partner requested. Lynx withdrew two sleeves filled with a fluorescent orange fluid and handed them over. "Got it," A.P. declared after a cursory examination. "The bubbles are intentional, so we just have to decode them. I'm afraid my translation algorithm for Farling is limited to the spoken language, though. I didn't want to pay extra for the written version. Does your ship library include alien scripts?"

"Display Farling character sets on the main viewer," Lynx said in her command voice, wondering whether the ship controller would have it in the reference library. Sure enough, a dense grid appeared, each square filled with a different arrangement of tiny spheres of varying sizes.

"This could be tougher than I thought if your ship can't read the labels directly," A.P. confessed. "It looks like they have thousands of characters, and I can barely differentiate between some of them."

117

"What we need is a junkie," Lynx commented. "When drugs are on the line, a junkie gets smart in a hurry."

"Does your ship include an ore analyzer for prospecting?" A.P. asked.

"It came with the standard package, but I've never had much use for it," Lynx replied, launching herself at the instrumentation suite. "I use the mass spectrometer for checking water, of course, since you can't survive long without one of those. There's an ore analyzer in the chamber beneath it and maybe they share some of the same test equipment. Ship. Is the ore analyzer functional?"

"Affirmative," the synthesized voice responded.

"Ship. Does it include a high resolution microscope?" A.P. inquired.

"Is the artificial person authorized to ask me questions?" the ship's controller inquired.

"Yes," Lynx replied. She hadn't consciously realized that she had been holding out on granting her partner access to the ship's voice control and he hadn't brought it up. Asking questions wasn't the same as giving orders, and she needed more time to get used to the idea of sharing her ship before she could go that far.

"The Braknest Mark IV ore analyzer includes a Gerft digital microscope."

"Can you filter the input of the microscope through your Farling symbol library for translation?" agent Malloy followed up.

"Unknown," the controller responded. "A test sample is required for analysis."

A.P. tossed a sleeve of the orange drug to Lynx, who fielded the throw like she was loading cargo and deposited it in the ore analyzer drawer. Before she could slide the drawer shut, A.P. added, "Ship. I'm asking for an optical

118

analysis of script on the sample only. Do not perform destructive mineral testing."

"Affirmative," the controller responded in a monotone, though Lynx imagined it sounded slightly disappointed, as if caught before it could play a trick. Most captains customized their ship controllers with personable voices, but Lynx had always found the practice spooky, and she knew more than one trader who had fallen into the habit of referring to his ship like a family member. The standard ship controllers weren't true AI. The controller just offered a natural language interface to the navigation console and instruments onboard, including the data in instruction manuals and a standard reference library. This could lead to the controllers sounding quite intelligent at times, but they weren't sentient.

"This is exciting!" Lynx beamed at her partner, then immediately regretted it. While examining a stash of drugs really was more exciting than anything she could recall doing while transiting a Stryx tunnel in the past, she was suddenly embarrassed to be telling it to an artificial person who no doubt thought that human lives were a nonstop adventure. She hoped she hadn't disappointed him.

"Persuasion," the ship controller intoned in its monotone. "Renders subject susceptible to new programming during effective period. Administer orally. See safety sheet for dosage and interactions."

"New programming?" Lynx asked hollowly. "For humans? I'll never take my eyes off my drink in a bar again!"

"You should never leave your drink unprotected in a bar regardless," A.P. told her. "The best solution would be if our employers provided a wide spectrum countermeasure or updated your implant with a drug detector. Shall we identify the rest of the samples?"

"I'm almost afraid to now," Lynx replied, shuddering as she removed the sleeve of Persuasion from the ore analyzer and floated it back to her partner. He caught the drug and returned it to the sack before tossing her a gently pulsing white sample. She fed it into the instrument and they waited.

"Zombie," the ship controller translated. "Permanent suppression of volition and ego, effects not reversible. Administer orally. See safety sheet for dosage and interactions."

"Safety sheet!" Lynx exploded. "They're selling chemical lobotomies and they're worried about dosage and interactions?"

"I'm sure whoever purchased such a drug would want to make sure it wasn't rendered ineffective if the victim was simultaneously taking cough medicine," A.P. suggested reasonably. "I think we have to presume that the safety sheets are intended for the buyer and not necessarily the final consumer."

"You know, we can't actually take these onto Corner Station," Lynx told A.P. after digesting the information. "If they're detected, the Stryx would confiscate my ship and hand us both over to EarthCent authorities, who would deny any knowledge of our mission. The Stryx don't allow these types of drugs on their stations."

"That doesn't prevent us from continuing with our assignment," A.P. replied. "Once we've cataloged the threats, we can simply dump the drugs in space or let the ore analyzer test them destructively. I believe that following the various imaging tests, the analyzer vaporizes rock samples for spectroscopic analysis. Perhaps there's

120

too much liquid in these, though. I think it would be safer to dump them."

"Toss me the red-and-white striped one," Lynx said grimly. "I want to know what all those people are taking for fun." She removed the zombie drug from the drawer and fed the analyzer the new sample to read. The wait was longer this time.

"Self-esteem," the controller announced finally. "Provides a sense of security and omniscience, combined with filtering optic nerve impulses for convergence. Suppresses cognitive functioning and logic centers. Administer orally or through dermal absorption. See safety sheet for dosage and interactions."

"I can understand the security and omniscience, alcohol does that too," Lynx ventured. "But what did the bit about filtering optical inputs mean, and how does suppressing logical thinking improve self-esteem? Oh wait, scratch that last part."

"By convergence, I'm guessing they mean that the drug reduces visual asymmetries through filtering the inputs from your binocular vision," A.P. ventured. "I don't know how they can pull that off, but if it works, it would lead most people who look in a mirror to believe that they're more attractive."

"Alcohol does that, too," Lynx observed. "Well, at least it doesn't say anything about mind control. Let's try the next color."

She removed the drug from the analyzer and zipped it over to A.P. in return for a sleeve full of inky black fluid. The two packets nearly collided mid-course, and Lynx suspected that her partner had aimed his on purpose, since he had released a second after she did. Well, tossing things back and forth in Zero-G was sort of fun, and anything beat listening to the descriptions of what some of these drugs could do to humans. She fed the new sample to the analyzer.

"Despair," the ship controller announced. "A broad spectrum depressant with overtones of anxiety and a hint of panic, combined with differential amplification of optic nerve impulses. Administer orally. See safety sheet for dosage and interactions."

"Differential amplification?" Lynx asked.

"If my previous surmise about filtering optic nerve impulses was correct, this would have the opposite effect," A.P. explained. "Rather than reducing visual asymmetries, it would increase them, making you believe your face was all out of proportion, that sort of thing."

"What did we ever do to the Farlings?" Lynx demanded. "It's bad enough that they're pushing an addictive recreational drug on humans, but three out of four of these samples have been downright evil."

"I doubt they harbor any ill will towards humanity in particular," her partner replied. "The Farlings no doubt manufacture similar drugs for all of the susceptible biologicals. They also manufacture some of the most effective medicines in the galaxy. It's just paying work to them."

"Are there any left?" Lynx asked. "I seem to remember a pretty blue one."

A.P. drew a sleeve filled with glowing blue fluid out of the bag and exchanged with Lynx. This time the two projectiles nicked each other midway, but the resulting change in trajectories wasn't enough to put either of them out of reach. Lynx shot her partner an annoyed look as she fielded the blue drug and inserted it in the assay drawer.

"Time travel," the controller read the drug's name from the Farling label. "Advances the biological clock with no known side effects. Administer orally or through dermal absorption. See safety sheet for dosage and interactions."

"Biologicals don't have clocks," Lynx protested as she retrieved the drug from the analyzer. "There must be an error in the translation."

"Of course you have clocks," A.P. told her. "Why do you think you get tired—hey, is that thing leaking?"

Lynx looked down at the transparent sleeve, and sure enough, a trail of tiny blue spheres extended behind it to the ore analyzer drawer, drifting slowly in Zero-G.

"You see what happens when you fool around throwing things back and forth?" she lectured her partner, holding the sleeve up between them. "The corner of the sleeve I was returning to you must have been just sharp enough to poke a tiny hole in this one."

"Just let go of it and back away, Lynx!" he told her urgently. "You don't want to get it on your skin."

Lynx blanched and let go of the sleeve immediately, her eyes darting back and forth for a safe path through the minefield of tiny blue spheres. Rather than retreating, she kicked off of the console and launched herself towards her command chair. In a blink of an eye, A.P. had the whole mess cleaned up and was strapped into the other chair.

"What happened?" Lynx asked. "How did you move so fast?"

"Oh, you're back," A.P. said cheerfully. "I put all the drugs in the disposal chute as soon as we came out of the tunnel. We're in a parking orbit around Corner Station."

"Out of the tunnel?" Lynx shrieked. "Are you telling me I've been asleep for days?"

"Was it that long?" her partner asked in wonder. "In any case, you weren't so much asleep as time traveling. I took advantage and got caught up on some of the old movies in the training materials and I'm thinking of changing my name to Smiley. Let me get that intravenous tube out of your arm before you start squirming around. Your ship controller was kind enough to inform me where the emergency medical supplies were located and how to use them. I had to give the bag a gentle squeeze once in a while since the Zero-G pump didn't work."

"How can you be so calm?" Lynx fought down her panic as she did a physical inventory, wiggling her fingers and toes and shaking her head to see if she was dizzy. A.P. removed the needle smoothly, as if he had been through emergency medical training at some point in his background. "I just got dosed with some alien drug that messed up my system clock!"

"See? I told you biologicals had clocks," A.P. replied complacently. "And good news, I've already received a hail from our contact. We can meet as soon as we dock at Corner Station."

"But I couldn't have absorbed more than one or two tiny droplets," Lynx said with a shudder. "What if a human drank the whole packet?"

"That would be a problem," her partner agreed. "But it could turn out to be a useful drug to stock for lifeboats that aren't equipped with stasis equipment. The ship's controller kept track of your vital signs and it appears that the drug triggered some form of latent hibernation, meaning your metabolism was greatly reduced. And if you're going to be in a temporary coma, Zero-G is a good place for it. No bedsores."

"You could at least apologize for fooling around with throwing the drugs back and forth!"

"I apologize for causing the sleeve to rupture," A.P. told her. "I also apologize for saving you a bundle on docking fees by remaining in a parking orbit, though of course, that was largely due to the fact that the ship controller won't accept my commands. If I understood its explanation, it would have allowed me to dock had you died, for which I'm grateful."

"You're forgiven," Lynx muttered, pulling up the time on her implant. Impossible as it seemed, they had entered the tunnel on Tuesday morning and it was now Sunday night. Five days of sleep? She called up the full calendar and gasped, "It's been twelve days!"

Twelve

"I'm sure you're all happy to see the little red padlock in the upper right-hand corner of your holograms," Home Boy said to begin the third meeting of EEK. "Thanks to a generous loan from our new director, code name 'Mercenary', this steering committee meeting will be encrypted. A special thanks to Toto, who recruited Mercenary, and who also hired Drazen Security Associates to sweep our respective offices of bugs before this meeting."

"They only did my personal office," Tinkerbelle complained. "When I asked about having the rest of the embassy swept, they said that would be extra."

"Did they check the other rooms?" Toto asked.

"Of course, that's their main sales tactic," the python-faced ambassador replied. "The rest of the place is lousy with bugs, but a detector only tells you there's active surveillance, it doesn't neutralize devices. Besides, I watched the Drazen tech working and he used some sort of projector to zap my office bugs in place. We'd have to tear the walls apart to get at them otherwise."

"If the bugs start coming back, we'll just have to find room in the budget to buy a bug-zapper," Troll added. "Otherwise, we're wasting creds paying for the secure channel."

126

"Agreed," Home Boy stated for the record. "Now, before we meet our management team, does anybody have any new business to suggest?"

"I do," Toto replied immediately. "We wrapped up the last meeting so suddenly that I didn't get a chance to tell you that our embassy is hosting a trade show for spies. The response has been overwhelming, probably because every alien intelligence service with a presence on Union Station was listening in when the show was planned. It's scheduled for the first three days of the next cycle, and I thought that some of you might want to attend or send a representative."

"Will there be any educational sessions?" Lion inquired.

"Only by way of the vendors," Toto replied. "It turns out that the manufacture and sale of espionage equipment is a big business in the galaxy, but tradecraft, the knowledge required to use the toys in the field, is closely guarded. It's one of the reasons our management team has decided to meet the Drazen intelligence head to establish inter-agency cooperation."

"Isn't that the sort of strategic decision that should have been reviewed by this committee first?" Mother asked.

"You tell them that," Toto replied dryly. "And then you can come up with the money to run an intelligence service."

"I, for one, am pleased that our new director is taking the initiative." Home Boy hastily inserted himself into the discussion. "And while I won't be attending the show myself, I agree that it's a good idea for as many of you as possible to gain some first-hand knowledge of what we're up against."

"I have a question," Pill Bottle said. "Now that we have a secure channel, why are we still using this zoo animals anonymity filter?"

"And as I reported previously, some of my alien counterparts have shown me recordings of our last meeting in which the animal scrambler was decoded and all of our faces were revealed," Troll added. "If this is the best security technology EarthCent has, we're in trouble."

"It's not exactly security technology," Home Boy admitted. "My grandson's school uses it for their home-study courses, just to liven things up for the kids. My team here thought it would be a good idea if you didn't all recognize each other for the sake of operational security. It was suggested along with the code names to be standard operating procedure."

"I think we could give up on the animal heads," Mother said.

"Unlike the Stryx, KinderZoo doesn't give partial refunds, so we may as well stick it out for today," Home Boy replied philosophically. "Is there anything else, or should Toto introduce our new sponsors, I mean, agency heads."

"Is there any news about the agents who were sent to investigate the Farling threat?" Tinkerbelle asked.

"We received a report they were in a parking orbit at Corner Station, but for some reason, they haven't contacted the embassy," Home Boy said. "It's the first subject I intend to broach with the new director."

"Where did you get the idea of sending them after the Farlings?" Lion asked. "Is there some ongoing intelligence gathering at HQ you haven't told us about?"

"We received an anonymous tip," Home Boy confessed. "It seemed credible because it was delivered with a small sample of a drug that would compel obedience. Since we didn't have any other training ideas, the mission to make a drug buy was a natural fit. Perhaps I was hasty."

"Did you test the drug?" Troll asked.

"On my wife's dog," Home Boy replied sadly. "For three weeks, he came when I called him, stopped barking when I told him to be quiet, and he even stayed off the couch."

"Did something go wrong?" Mother asked sympathetically.

"Yes, I used up the sample," Home Boy said with a tragic air. "I'm sure he remembers the whole thing and holds it against me, because now he's worse than he was before."

"Serves you right," barked the Cairn terrier. "It's a good thing you aren't coming to the show, because I have a two-hundred-pound dog that doesn't take kindly to mind control."

"I'll keep that in mind, Toto," Home Boy replied mildly. "Now, if there are no further objections, shall we meet the new heads of our intelligence agency?"

The hologram projected from the display desk winked, and suddenly Clive and Blythe appeared, sitting on the bridge of a decidedly alien ship.

"My code name was Mercenary," Clive announced. He paused to take in all of the animal heads and make the mental association with the diplomats they concealed, thanks to a cheat sheet provided by the Drazens. "Due to our early lack of operational security, everybody involved in intelligence work not attending this meeting already knows that my name is Clive Oxford, so you may as well just call me Clive."

"My code name is Control," Blythe said in a voice that implied she meant it. With her hair pulled back in a tight bun and strategic use of make-up, she looked closer to thirty than twenty. "I've met most of you in person over the last three years so you probably recognize me as the co-owner of InstaSitter, but I'm sticking with Control because I like it. Although we have every confidence in Stryx encryption, it would serve no purpose to discuss specific details that you don't require for oversight purposes. Subject to that condition, we are ready to answer any questions you may have."

"I'd like to personally express my gratitude to you for accepting the job with its associated expenses," Home Boy thanked the Oxfords. "Speaking of those expenses, would it violate your conditions to say something about the scale of your initial operations?"

"Our plan, which requires your cooperation, includes funding a cultural attaché position at all of the EarthCent embassies on Stryx stations." Clive waited a moment to see if there would be a protest, even though Blythe had assured him the committee would agree to anything that came with funding. "The attaché will serve as a liaison with the ambassador, as well as providing local control or point of contact for agents in the vicinity. We have already begun recruiting agents and information analysts on a large scale, with the initial goal of maintaining one full-time agent in the field for every analyst at headquarters. The basic approach is to pair each analyst with an agent in a flat hierarchy, which will maximize our coverage during the start-up phase when we hardly know where we need to be concentrating our resources."

"Will the cultural attachés count as agents?" Tinkerbelle asked.

"No," Clive responded. "In addition to liaison and point-of-contact duties, the cultural attachés will be expected to spend as much time as possible socializing with the local species, especially those with whom EarthCent has yet to form official relations. There may be some overlap with regular embassy activities, so we'll need to work out the kinks as we go along. In essence, we want to systematically build our institutional knowledge of alien cultures based on first-hand observations, rather than relying on media and Stryx reference materials."

"So they actually will be functioning as cultural attachés, sort-of," Toto observed. "Will this information be shared with the local embassy?"

"All reports produced by the cultural attachés will be submitted to the local embassy, EarthCent HQ and EarthCent Intelligence," Blythe replied. "But their activities as point-of-contact, support, and control of local agents will only be reported to us."

"Well, that sounds like a pretty ambitious program to start," Troll said. "I think it will be a great benefit to the embassies to have a staff member who is dedicated to learning about some of the less-than-forthcoming aliens, even if it's just part-time. Practically all of our limited resources go into providing what support services we can for transient humans while keeping up appearances with the other species."

"In addition to the three types of full-time staffers we've talked about and a thin layer of management, we've established a training center for all personnel. Our initial recruits will receive instruction in tradecraft and some basic self-defense skills, primarily for the sake of team-building and creating confidence in the program," Clive continued. "We may bring in some promising stringers for training as well, though for the time being, the field agents who run them will have to teach them any necessary tradecraft."

"I've followed along pretty well up to this point, and I'm deeply impressed by both your plan and your willingness to finance such a large operation," Home Boy interjected. "In fact, it goes far beyond what I imagined might be possible. But I lost you on agents running stringers."

"Stringers in the journalistic or intelligence world are also known as casuals," Blythe explained. "They'll be humans who are sympathetic with our goals and who may be paid for piece-work, but they'll have their own careers or occupations outside of our agency, and they may go for years at a time without producing any intelligence of note. Our field agents will focus on creating networks of independent traders and bartenders, who tend to hear the latest rumors, but they'll also enlist humans who live in or travel to places where we have a need for information. Currently, if a human sees something that could be vital to our interests, all they can do is gossip about it. We want everyone to know that there's a new human agency that wants to hear about what's going on out there, and may even pay them for their trouble."

"It sounds a little like you're trying to recruit all of humanity to serve as spies," Mother complained. "Isn't this what they call mission creep?"

"I don't see why we need to worry about scope as long as they're willing to pay for it," Troll pointed out.

"We're not trying to recruit all of humanity," Clive assured Mother. "And we don't have infinite funds, something my wife will address in a moment. But there's a big difference between operating an intelligence agency on a galactic scale and the old national espionage services that flourished on Earth a century ago. Since EarthCent lacks a military, we can't piggyback on their resources or draw from their ranks for agents. And since the only successful human entertainment channels are focused on sports programming, we can't rely on foreign correspondents or investigative reporters to provide early warnings of intergalactic developments. The first analysts we hired are already learning how to monitor the alien news feeds around the clock, but of course, that's mainly valuable as a barometer of how the more important species are getting along."

"It took me three decades of reading reports from our ambassadors to learn that lesson," Home Boy concurred. "No matter how important an event might be to us, we're just a small, primitive species without an empire, a military, or the cure for the common cold. The only human event to lead the galactic news in the forty-three years I've worked for EarthCent was the auction of Kasilian treasures held on Union Station last year."

"Did I hear something about your funding running into limitations already?" Troll asked cautiously. "We really hoped that the Intelligence branch might become self-funding through the trading activity of its agents."

"Let me address that question," Blythe replied, looking somewhat irritated for the first time. "I understand that EarthCent has been functioning under tremendous fiscal constraints, but recruiting traders to use their own ships and skills to support themselves while functioning as career agents is neither viable nor ethical. All career EarthCent Intelligence personnel recruited on my watch will receive both a salary and matching contributions to Stryx-managed retirement funds. If they use their own spaceships in the course of their work, we will pay expenses and depreciation."

"I don't understand," Home Boy objected. "Unless you're hoping to convince the Stryx to provide funding, how long can you hope to carry the expenses yourselves?"

"Do you all remember the Raider/Trader craze of a few years ago?" Blythe asked in reply to his question.

The ambassadors replied with a chorus of, "Sure," "Unfortunately," and "Hated it."

"After the hype about military confrontations died down and most of the young men quit playing, the Trader part of the game continued to have great success, and it still draws tens of millions of new players from most of the known species every cycle. The reason the Verlocks subsidize the real-time tunneling communications charges that make the game possible is that they are cleaning up on selling market data to trading concerns across the galaxy."

"So you intend to go into competition with the Verlocks?" Pill Bottle asked. "I've had pretty extensive dealings with them over the years, and I can assure you that they would view such competition as an act of aggression."

"No, the game is their rice bowl," Blythe replied. "It's also a bigger and much more complex business than we're capable of launching or funding at this time. But we do intend to develop commercially viable intelligence products and sell that information to businesses. Once we've built out our network of human resources, we may also experiment with selling courier and security services for human businesses, in addition to the standard industrial espionage."

"I'm not sure I like where this is headed," Mother cautioned. "You're telling me that we're going to be actively trying to steal industrial secrets from the other species?"

"Absolutely," Blythe replied. "Any industrial espionage we can manage on our own will be fine by the Stryx, and the other species as well, for that matter. Most of them are engaged in proxy wars, using economic output in the place of fleets and weapons. Yes, many of the advanced species have space armadas and one day humanity will likely need one as well, but that's primarily to ensure the safety of their merchants and explorers outside of Stryx space. And it's why sending a couple of untrained agents into Farling space was not a bright beginning for our agency."

"Their instructions specifically prohibited them from going deeper into Farling space than the overlap at the Stryx tunnel exit," Home Boy protested.

"We understand that, but those border volumes of space, where there's a tunnel termination but no station, aren't really viewed as Stryx space," Clive responded. "The Farlings certainly wouldn't do anything that would anger the Stryx, like preventing a ship from entering the tunnel, but you have to remember that the Farlings don't live under observation like we do on the stations. What happens in Farling space is their business. That's why they can manufacture and sell harmful drugs that are illegal on Stryx stations."

"I am worried about those agents and I accept full responsibility if something has gone wrong," Home Boy stated.

"We are currently on our way to Corner Station to meet our stray agents and bring them in," Clive replied. "Our information suggests that they are fine, but that they encountered an unexpected delay."

"Unexpected advance," Blythe corrected him.

"Well, this was all very interesting," Lion said. "Shouldn't we vote on accepting cultural attachés since it affects us directly?"

"Good point," Troll seconded the idea. "We are a committee after all."

"Very well," Home Boy concurred. "All in favor of accepting a cultural attaché who will be recruited and paid by EarthCent Intelligence, raise your hand. One, two, three, four, five, six, seven, eight, nine. Very good. For the record, that's seven in favor, none opposed. Only sitting committee members get to vote."

"Fine," Blythe said sharply. "Just wait and see if we invite you to any of our committee meetings."

"I think somebody should point out that we are putting a lot of eggs in the Union Station basket," Mother said. "The trade show, the spy school, it's even the home office for our generous new management team."

"We got a deal on the rental for the training camp, and a part-time instructor as well," Blythe reported. "Of course, if you have an equivalent facility you'd be willing to pay for..."

"I was just pointing it out," Mother replied meekly. "I think Union Station is a wonderful choice."

"So I see no reason to reconvene this committee before there's something important to discuss," Home Boy concluded, his mind on Blythe's private admonition that she wouldn't pay for a secure channel every month. "I suggest we meet after the trade show on Union Station takes place, and perhaps some of you who attend will have a chance to meet in person."

"And I'm looking forward to seeing you all next time without the animal heads," Mother added, as time ran out and the holograms dissolved.

Thirteen

Lynx was still a little unsteady on her feet following nearly two weeks of comatose inactivity in Zero-G, but after sucking down a couple tubes of protein-fortified fruit juice, she felt ready to face the world. Well, she admitted to herself, maybe not the world, but at least their contact man. A.P. told her that a short time before she woke up, they had received an open transmission inviting them to attend an auction at the Corner Station convention center. Since the invitation purportedly came from Lynx's grandmother, A.P. assumed that it was sent by their contact and not a random advertisement.

Chance benefitted from Lynx's extended vacation from consciousness because it allowed her time to reconstitute her dead back-up cell to the point that it would keep her on her feet for a few days without needing to swill a bottle of high-proof booze for fuel every couple hours. A.P. revived Chance when the Prudence broke parking orbit to approach the station, and she immediately contacted the Stryx AI administration to begin negotiations for financing a new power pack.

"They want me to get a job," Chance complained to Lynx when the two of them met on the bridge. The Stryx station manager had just taken over navigation and was guiding the ship towards a docking berth on the core. The feeling of gravity slowly increased as Corner Station's

137

manipulator fields began spinning the ship around the axis of the core to match the station's rotational velocity. "I'm not the kind of artificial person who can punch a clock, you know. I have to be free. What difference does it make to them if I'm a few years behind on the mortgage payments for this body? They know I'm good for it."

"Have you ever made a payment?" A.P. inquired.

"I almost did, once," Chance said defensively. "But there was this hat I just had to buy, you should have seen me in it. Man, I wish I knew what happened to that hat," she added mournfully.

"How long has it been since you were recognized as a sentient being?" Lynx asked curiously.

"Six years, two months, thirteen days, nine hours, fourteen minutes," Chance responded immediately. "I could give you a more accurate time if I had access to your implant, but I can't speak quickly enough to get the seconds right."

"How about you, partner?" Lynx followed up.

"Oh, it's been a while," A.P. replied vaguely. "I've never missed a payment because I let the Stryx pull the money from my account. In fact, I paid off my first body well ahead of schedule."

"Whoop-de-do," Chance mumbled.

"I don't get how you could just ignore your payments like that," A.P. admonished her. "You gave the Stryx your word of honor when you accepted the money. Without them, you'd just be running as a program in some crude human-built robot, and it would take you all day to answer a question like, 'What's your favorite color?'"

"Silver," Chance replied sulkily. "You don't have to lecture me, I got enough of that from the Stryx before I left their space. I just get bored, you know?"

138

"What kind of job do you think you'd like?" Lynx asked the artificial person. Chance was beginning to remind her of some adolescent girls she used to hang out with in the casino food courts while her father made a living at the tables.

"I don't know, maybe something in fashion?" Chance replied, winding a lock of long hair onto her index finger. Lynx pictured her chewing gum at the same time and couldn't help smiling.

"Docking sequence completed," the Stryx station manager announced over the ship's comm. "Welcome to the business class facility of Corner Station. Nose filters are not necessary in your docking area as long as you remain in the sections designated with a green stripe. A full service inspection is scheduled for 11:45 AM, local human time."

"Business class? Full service inspection?" Lynx responded incredulously. "I don't have that kind of creds. Is it too late to move us to the trader dock without incurring charges?"

"Your docking fees and maintenance have been prepaid," the Stryx informed her. "However, if you wish to be moved and skip the service…"

"No, business class is fine," Lynx amended herself hastily. Things were definitely looking up.

When A.P. and Lynx headed out for the convention center to make contact, Chance tagged along without any discussion. She was about the same size as Lynx, who loaned the artificial person a slinky dress that she'd bought on impulse and then never had the courage to wear. Chance made it look so good that Lynx decided on the spot not to ask for it back. Given the artificial person's

139

track record with loans, it was doubtful that Chance would think to return it of her own accord.

The auction was finished by the time they arrived, and Lynx worried that they had missed their contact opportunity, but a Horten girl ran up to them the moment they entered the hall. She pulled a Horten display cloth out of her sleeve, shook it out, and held it up to compare the image with Lynx's face.

"I got Lynx!" the girl shouted, pointing as if she was identifying a bidder.

"Bring her down," a human woman hollered back from the central stage, which was cluttered with merchandise that either hadn't met the minimum or had been purchased by remote bidders and needed to be packaged for delivery.

"You just earned me a fifty-cred bonus," the Horten girl informed them joyfully. When Lynx stared at her dumbfounded, the girl asked, "What's the matter? Isn't your translation implant working?"

"Sorry, I didn't mean to ignore you," Lynx replied. "I just didn't expect such a public welcome."

"I've been working as a spotter at the auction for the last week and they told us to expect you the first day," the girl informed her. The new arrivals and their Horten guide walked down the aisle, avoiding the stragglers who were moaning to each other about how much they would have bid if the auctioneers had just given them a little more time to think. "After you didn't show, they raised the bonus and pushed your picture out to all of the InstaSitters on the station. Did you run away from home or something?"

"I'm a grown-up!" Lynx replied indignantly, but that didn't seem to impress the girl. "No, I didn't run away from home. I've been, uh, resting."

A small woman who looked about Lynx's age met them at the edge of the stage and handed the Horten a fifty-cred coin. "Thanks, G'shell, we were beginning to worry," she told the girl before addressing the newcomers. "I'm Shaina, and that's my sister Brinda over there. Some friends of ours asked us to meet you and keep you here until they could arrive. Of course, you spent so long parked in orbit that we almost missed you."

"You did the Kasilian auction!" Chance exclaimed, practically glowing with excitement. "All of that beautiful jewelry. I'm Chance and I need a job. Are you hiring?"

"Pleased to meet you, Chance," Shaina replied. "We might be hiring, but as you can see from some of the leftover lots, the Kasilian auction was a once-in-a-lifetime event for a very long-lived species. We've been covering our expenses doing a circuit of the stations, but it's still touch and go. This auction would have been a loss if my sister hadn't recognized that some antique holo recordings included the earliest known performance of Grvat Haledy, which added nearly sixty thousand to the gross sales."

"I like the idea of traveling on a circuit," Chance replied, quickly getting over any disappointment that the auction business wasn't all jewelry and more jewelry. "Do you have your own ship?"

"We've been renting," Shaina admitted. "It's just a small business, my sister and I, plus our partner, Jeeves. We use InstaSitters for auction spotters and presenters. Do you have any special talents?"

"I'm friendly," Chance told her brightly. "I've earned drinks at bars all over the galaxy by bringing in customers."

"A useful skill, no doubt," Jeeves said, floating up to Shaina's side. "But isn't a certain artificial person we know approximately six years, one month, thirteen days, nine hours and fifty minutes behind on her first mortgage payment?"

"There's nothing I hate more than a robot gossip," Chance replied with a pout. "Besides, how am I ever going to start paying if being a little late on my mortgage means I can't find a job?"

"Fortunately for you, the AI administration accepts payment through wage garnishment," Jeeves informed her. "If you come to work for SBJ Auctioneers, fifty percent of your pay will be applied directly to your outstanding debt."

"I'll agree if you roll in the overhaul loan I just negotiated," Chance counter-offered, showing an unexpected talent for bargaining. "I really need the new power cell. All of the humanoids think I'm a lush."

"Agreed," Jeeves answered. "Someday I'll be interested in hearing how you managed to ruin your original power cell and back-up so quickly, but we have to be on our way as soon as possible. I just notified the AI administration you've accepted employment with us, so run along and have yourself maintained, and I'll send you our departure details when they're finalized."

"Thanks for everything," Chance replied happily, dropping a curtsy to A.P. and Lynx. Without further ado, she sashayed back up the aisle towards the exit, drawing admiring looks from the few humanoids left in the seating sections. Lynx watched her dress disappear with equal measures of regret and relief. She wasn't sure how much more of Chance's bubbly personality she could take when her own career was up in the air.

"What are we going to do with her?" Shaina asked Jeeves, somewhat surprised by the Stryx's sudden offer of employment.

"If she doesn't work out, we'll pass her onto Blythe," Jeeves replied.

"Are you kidding?" Shaina asked. "The last thing InstaSitter needs is a delinquent buy-me-drinkee girl as a babysitter, even if she is an artificial person."

"Not for InstaSitter," Jeeves said in a conspiratorial tone. "A twenty-four-hour bargirl would be an asset in Blythe's new business."

"I thought you weren't supposed to know about that," Shaina replied in a stage whisper, glancing mischievously at the waiting EarthCent Intelligence agents as she spoke.

"We aren't supposed to take sides," Jeeves said. "That's not the same thing as closing our eyes as if we didn't know what's going on. In fact, I'm told the Effterii just docked, so you'll be hearing from the great spymaster herself shortly. And I'll admit that I'm looking forward to the Union Station espionage show. Pays to keep a watch on the biologicals."

"Excuse me," Lynx interrupted, eying the auctioneers. "I wasn't trying to, uh, spy on you, but between the Horten girl with my picture and what the two of you just said, I can't help wondering if my cover is blown."

"Only in intelligence circles," Jeeves answered, which wasn't as reassuring to Lynx as he might have intended. "Your employers suffered from certain operational problems at the time you were hired, nothing out of the ordinary for a brand new agency. Fortunately, there was a change of management, and we all have great confidence in the new team."

"Are you really a spy?" Shaina asked with obvious interest. "I've never met a spy before, or at least, not one who admitted to it. I'm thinking of signing up myself. I have the perfect cover for making the rounds of the stations, meeting different people and handling all sorts of merchandise."

"Should you be saying that out loud?" Lynx asked, flicking her eyes towards Jeeves.

"Because of Jeeves?" Shaina said, and burst out laughing. "You can't keep anything from the Stryx, at least not on the stations, and probably not anywhere if you're using their ship controllers, registers, or implants. They must be the nosiest sentients the galaxy has ever seen."

"Well-informed sentients," Jeeves corrected her.

"Hey, are you guys interested in eating something?" Brinda called from across the stage. "There's a food court just above the reception hall that has a pizza place I've been meaning to try. I'll pay if you'll walk."

"Deal," Lynx hollered back. "I can use the exercise and the solid food. What do you want on it?"

"We eat everything," Shaina told her, casually catching the fifty-cred coin that Brinda threw to her like a missile, and handing it to Lynx. "Get the party size if they make one. Can't have too much cold pizza on a tunnel trip. It sticks together in Zero-G."

"Are you coming, A.P.?" Lynx asked her partner.

"You go ahead," A.P. replied. "I'll help them pack while I catch up with Jeeves."

Lynx found the pizza place in the food court and ordered a party combination. She thought about walking a few laps around the corridors while the pizza baked, but in the end, she gave in to her loss of muscle tone and just sat in a booth to wait.

144

Twenty minutes later, she was on her way back to the auction hall, carefully carrying the over-sized pizza box in front of her. Fortunately, the pizza place used alien technology for the insulator at the bottom of the box, so it remained stiff, and she didn't have to wrap her fingers in something to keep them from burning. Lynx had meant to spend the wait preparing to meet her new boss and report on their mission to Farling Seventy, but instead she had spaced out, watching a rebroadcast of a Zero-G cage-fighting tournament from years before. She seemed to remember losing money on the match, betting on a man who wore green tights. Never bet on a man wearing green tights, she reminded herself.

At the entrance to the hall where she'd been intercepted by the Horten girl a half an hour earlier, Lynx was met by a human couple. The man took the pizza box from her with a friendly nod and headed down towards the stage, while the young woman stopped her from following.

"You're Lynx," Blythe said, examining EarthCent Intelligence's first human agent from head to toe. "I'm Control. Are you all right? The first thing we did when we took over the agency was to attempt to locate you. They never should have sent you on a mission outside of Stryx space without training."

"You're my new boss?" Lynx asked in surprise. "You're younger than me!"

"My husband is the new agency director, if that makes you feel any better," Blythe replied, not unsympathetically. "Come on. Let's eat, and then we can talk shop."

"I have a question about that," Lynx muttered in an undertone as they headed down the aisle to the stage. "All of these people seem to be, well, in on it, if you know what I mean. The contact I had with the old director on Earth and the impression I got from the training materials seemed to indicate that spying should be, well, secret."

"We're all old friends, and with Jeeves around, it's safer to talk here than anywhere other than on my husband's ship," Blythe replied in her normal tone of voice. "Did Thomas tell you that he worked with me for years?"

"Who's Thomas?" Lynx asked as they reached the stage. The box was already open on the floor and three slices were missing. Clive and Blythe had agreed ahead of time to let her handle the introduction with Lynx, so he hadn't wasted any time starting in on the pizza with the Hadads.

"Your partner," Blythe replied, helping herself to a slice. "You've been working together for nearly a month and you didn't tell her about me, Thomas?"

"First of all, she was unconscious half the time," A.P. replied, holding up a hand and ticking off a finger. "Second of all, we barely talked on the tunnel trip out because I stayed in the hold, so she wouldn't feel like I was trying to take over her ship. Third, my prior employment just didn't come up."

"You told me that most of your recent experience was in supervisory positions," Lynx reminded him, after swallowing a bite of salty pizza.

"That's absolutely accurate," Blythe said, picking the onions off of her own slice and putting them on her husband's. "Thomas was our top employee for almost four years. How many different species did you sit for, Thomas?"

"Eighty-two, if you count Gem as a species," Thomas replied.

"Sit for?" Lynx repeated, something that was getting to be a habit with her when her partner was around. "And how did you get from A.P. to Thomas?"

"Thomas really is my name, but they got it wrong in the EarthCent file, just like you got listed as Hedgehouse," he explained. "I filled out the application as Artificial Person Thomas Malloy, but the Old Man called me A.P., and when I peeked at my folder in the reflection from his watch, I saw that they had me down as A.P. Thomas Malloy. If I had known they were going to do that, it would have saved me the effort of making up a last name, and I would have been A.P. Thomas."

"We fixed it already, for both of you," Blythe said. "How did you come up with Malloy?"

"It's a contraction for Mobile Alloy," Thomas explained. "I'm mobile, and an alloy is at least two kinds of metal combined with at least one non-metal substance, so I thought it was descriptive and would be easy to remember."

"You were a mobile alloy babysitter?" Lynx asked, unable to let go of the supervisory claim so easily.

"I was a mobile alloy InstaSitter," Thomas replied proudly. "The best of the best of the best. I never lost a client, though I did let the first human girl I supervised stay up after her bedtime."

"My sister and I started InstaSitter, and it's paying the bills for EarthCent Intelligence for the time being," Blythe explained to Lynx. "I'm sure you'll be happy to hear that we're dropping the 'Pay yourself and your partner out of your trading profits,' idea. You'll be on straight salary and we'll pay any ship expenses for missions that we assign. Your trading profits are always your own."

"Forget that you're younger than me," Lynx blurted. "I mean, you're still younger than me, but I don't care anymore. How about the initial cargo that EarthCent provided for us at the elevator anchor? The truth is, I was nearly broke at the time, and it seems like a mad scientist was responsible for loading the container. It wasn't going to make us rich, but there was certainly something for every situation."

"They took up a collection from the local EarthCent staff and added some unclaimed freight from the warehouse," Blythe told her. "Apparently, some of the EarthCent employees took it as an opportunity to clean out their closets or their garages. By the way, somebody claims they gave away their family's heirloom silver by mistake, so if you haven't traded it yet, we should return it."

"We still have it," Lynx confessed. "Too bad, it was the nicest item, though there was some high-end liquor that's worth good creds."

"We hear there was a bit of a crisis back at headquarters over that as well," Blythe told her with a laugh. "Apparently, some spouses saw your need for tradable goods as an opportunity to engage in behavioral modification. Good luck to them."

"So you had a chance to go through my file and you're still keeping me?" Lynx asked.

"There really wasn't anything in your file when we took possession," Blythe replied, as she denuded another slice of offensive onion bits. "Just a note saying you owned your ship free and clear, and several images of you that looked like they were taken through somebody's implant in a bar setting. I had the InstaSitter personnel department run a background check and you did fine. Come to think of it, we probably need to loosen our standards for hiring spies. The work isn't as sensitive as supervising children and old people."

"Would you be interested in another artificial person as an agent?" Thomas spoke up. "Jeeves hired her for the auction business because she needed a job to get a new loan, but I think she'd do better in a less structured environment."

"Are you talking about Chance?" Blythe asked, her face breaking into a wide grin. "That girl is unique. Sure, we'll hire her. I persuaded Stryx Farth to send me your passenger list when you entered parking orbit around his station, and we checked on her background as well. Unlike most human developed AI's who come out of the Open University programs on the stations, Chance was conceived and coded on Earth. Apparently, the remaining fraternities and sororities thought that creating an artificial intelligence would be a good way to prove their relevancy in the modern age, but it took them nearly sixty years to get her past the Turing/Ryskoff test."

"Frat boys and sorority girls, that explains a lot," Lynx said. "But I have to admit, she made our mission a success. Can I, uh, talk about that here?"

"Yes, and as somebody who has spent a lot of time traveling in deep space, I'm curious to hear about your enforced hibernation," Clive said, after surreptitiously spitting something out into a napkin. Onions didn't really agree with him either, but they were still working on that facet of the marriage.

"The Farlings are manufacturing and selling drugs that would be incredibly harmful to humans, way beyond the recreational stuff," Lynx told them. "They had drugs to turn humans into permanent zombies and drugs that allow humans to be temporarily controlled. The drug that I

149

got accidentally dosed with just from handling the sleeve was described as a time travel drug. And I swear, it didn't feel like a second went by, but I was out for twelve days!"

"It really didn't seem that long," Thomas added mildly, drawing a glare from his partner.

"Don't pay attention to him," Blythe advised Lynx. "He has issues with times and dates."

"Well, I felt fine afterwards. Just hungry, thanks to, uh, Thomas fixing me up with emergency fluids," Lynx continued. "According to the ship controller, my metabolism was slowed down so much that it was barely detectable. So I guess that was a pretty useful drug, but Thomas got rid of it all when we came out of the tunnel."

"The drugs are being analyzed," Jeeves informed them. "Farth saw the ejection, of course, and after clarifying the situation with Thomas, he sent a bot to retrieve some crystals, since the packages all ruptured in the vacuum. We won't divulge pharmaceutical trade secrets, but we keep track of the types of drugs we ban from our stations to make it easier to detect them."

"I don't know how you keep all your noninterference rules straight," Blythe complained. "It seems to me like you make them up as you go along."

"I wouldn't repeat this to the older Stryx, but it's mainly a question of appearances," Jeeves told her. "You know the old riddle about who polices the police?"

"Nobody?" Lynx ventured.

"Exactly," Jeeves replied, allowing the self-satisfaction to show in his synthesized voice. "It's a hard job, but somebody has to do it."

"We also took some surveillance photographs of suspicious activities on the surface of Seventy," Thomas said. "Lynx was very daring."

"Photographs?" Clive asked. "I think I've seen some prints in a gallery, the old chemical process, right? When can we look at them?"

"It'll be a while," Lynx explained defensively. "I want to use up the roll before I send it for developing."

Fourteen

The ragged line of approximately two dozen humans, male and female, stood more or less at attention in the newly designated parade grounds at Mac's Bones. While the camping and repair business was still going tolerably well, it had never made full use of the space left in the hold after consolidating the old Raider/Trader mock-ups into cabins and losing the parking business for Paul's old gaming squadron. When Clive brought up the subject of establishing a training camp for the new intelligence service, Joe had jumped at the opportunity. Then Clive drafted him to help with the training.

"You are the first class of EarthCent Intelligence agents attending our new training facility, so we'll be feeling our way forward together," Clive began his speech. He stood before the recruits at parade rest with his hands held behind his back. "You've all passed the same vetting and expressed your desire to serve humanity, and I want to make clear that in intelligence work, your main weapon will be your brain. That said, we'll be starting with a course in self-defense, taught by myself and instructor Joe McAllister. The goal is not to encourage you to insert yourself into situations where you'll need to fight for your life, but rather to give you the confidence so you won't get backed into a corner."

"Could I interrupt?" asked a bookish-looking middle-aged man from the line, half raising his hand.

"I haven't gotten to the part about discipline yet, so go ahead," Clive replied with a wry smile.

"I was recruited as an analyst, and I was told I wouldn't need to leave Union Station," the man said. "It's not that I'm against learning a little self-defense, but I have a wife and four children, so I'm really not interested in a job that would take me away from the station."

"The majority of you here today are on track to become analysts or cultural attachés," Clive responded. "We have no intention of asking the analysts to go on missions, or of asking the field agents to stay up all night reading, for that matter. But you will eventually be paired as teams, an analyst for every field agent, and taking physical training together is an important exercise for team building."

"How about partners?" Lynx asked, without raising her hand. "Will partners in the field share a single analyst?"

"So everybody, this is Lynx," Clive said, beckoning her to step out from the line. "Lynx, this is everybody. Lynx was one of the first two agents recruited by EarthCent before I became the director, and she volunteered to audit the training course, even though she has already successfully completed a mission in the field. Lynx is a trader by profession, and she was assigned an artificial person as a partner by the previous management. In short, the answer to her question is that field agent teams will be partnered with a single analyst. Thank you, Lynx."

Lynx nodded and stepped back into the line, where the man next to her immediately whispered out of the side of his mouth, "You were on a real mission? Where did you go?"

"Shh!" Lynx replied, keeping her eyes fixed on Clive. She had never gone to camp as a child and she was trying to make the most out of the experience.

"I'm not going to give you a pep talk or tell you about the importance of your work for humanity," Clive continued. "My own service background was in the mercenaries, where money and remaining alive were the only measures of success. Most of your work in intelligence will be more akin to journalism than anything of a military nature, though unlike journalists, you'll be reporting to a private audience. Which leads me to our most important rule. The information gathered by field agents and assessed by analysts will be kept private. No sharing with your friends or family, and this is an absolute condition of employment. You're welcome to tell everybody that you work for EarthCent Intelligence, it may help us with recruiting, but you will treat the intelligence we generate like proprietary business secrets. Any questions so far?"

"What's that thing sneaking up behind you?" asked a young woman, one of several recruits Blythe had brought in from InstaSitter's human alumni.

Clive spun around striking a defensive pose, but then relaxed just as quickly when he saw it was Beowulf. "This is Beowulf, and he'll be keeping an eye on the training. He's part Huravian, a war dog with more combat experience than most career mercenaries, though he's been retired for some years now."

Beowulf yawned at Clive to show he wasn't insulted by this last comment, displaying a mouth full of formidable, if well-worn, teeth. Then he strutted forward stiffly, like an old general reviewing the troops, the arthritis in his hips giving him a military gait that impressed the recruits as he

154

walked down their line. When he reached Lynx, the hair on his back bristled and he gave a deep-throated growl. The man next to EarthCent's first human agent began to tremble and back away. With one lunge, Beowulf put the man on his back and pinned him to the deck.

"Hold him, boy!" Joe shouted. He charged forward towards the dog and the downed recruit, with Clive just a step behind. "What have you got?"

Beowulf growled again, his massive head just inches away from his captive's face. The man's features were twitching violently, almost as if he had two different faces, and when Lynx got over her initial shock, she realized she'd seen such a performance before.

"He's a Vergallian face dancer!" she exclaimed, pointing down at the man as the recruits backed away to a safe distance. "I once saw a face dancer in a bar get drunk and lose his concentration and he got all twitchy like that."

"Vergallian!" Joe growled, almost as deeply as Beowulf as he stood over the fallen alien. "Got any last words?"

"Get him off me, get him off me. I'll talk, I'll talk," the Vergallian cried in fear. "They didn't say anything about a monster dog."

"Talk first and then I'll get him off you," Joe replied, as the Vergallian tried to avoid a descending dollop of dog drool without success. "Where's the man you're impersonating."

"They have him in stasis," the Vergallian practically sobbed out the reply. "If anything happens to me, you'll never get him back."

"You know that kidnapping is a capital crime in EarthCent jurisdiction?" Clive interjected, not having a clue whether or not it was true. "The Stryx don't interfere with local law enforcement."

"He wasn't kidnapped," the alien babbled. "He chose to follow a woman into the Vergallian section where he made inappropriate advances."

"No human chooses to follow a Vergallian woman anywhere," Joe retorted. "You're not giving me any reasons to keep the dog from making you his dinner."

"I have a swap card, I have a swap card," the Vergallian shouted in panic. "Let me get it out. I swear you'll get your man back unharmed."

"A swap card?" Joe asked, squatting down on his haunches to stare into the alien's eyes. "What's that?"

"Just get the dog off of me, I'll explain everything," the Vergallian moaned, beginning to froth at the mouth.

Joe exchanged glances with Clive and then reluctantly ordered the dog, "Down, boy!" Beowulf interpreted the instruction as a reason to drop his entire bulk onto the Vergallian's chest, forcing the air from his lungs in an explosive gasp. "Come on, you know that I know that you know that's not what I meant," Joe reasoned with the dog. "You did a good job, now get off of him and you can have an extra beer before bedtime."

Beowulf rolled off of the Vergallian and onto his side, taking his time in the process, then slowly rose to his feet, throwing in a down-dog stretch just to show he couldn't be hurried. The alien, who had begun to turn white, remained on his back, but recovered his poise quickly.

"That was torture!" he exclaimed. "The Treaty of Gersh prohibits torture of captive intelligence agents who identify themselves and offer a swap card."

"The Treaty of Gersh. I don't think I've ever heard of that one," Clive remarked to Joe. "You?"

"I sort of remember a general back on Hwoult Five referring to it when he was telling me about the history of the planet," Joe replied. "It's nothing we've ever signed."

"Everybody signs the Treaty of Gersh!" the Vergallian agent declared in alarm. "You have to! How can you run an intelligence service and not sign the Treaty of Gersh! I demand to see a whachamacallit, an attorney. Do you think I'd be stupid enough to accept this mission without the treaty protections?"

"Apparently you are," Clive pointed out. "And you had plenty of time to figure out for yourself that we couldn't have signed back when you were studying on Earth to pass as human."

The Vergallian agent blanched as if Beowulf had just collapsed on his chest again. "How did you know? Wait, I have a right to remain silent!"

"Your only right is to be eaten by a dog," Joe informed him in a steely voice. "You seem to be confusing Earth with EarthCent, we have different sets of rules. If you don't want to talk, you can scream."

"No, I'll talk, I'll talk," the Vergallian repeated frantically. "Under the Treaty of Gersh, undercover agents impersonating an alien all carry a swap card to expedite an exchange if they get caught. Nobody would do this work otherwise."

"Explain how the swap card works," Clive ordered. More than anything else to this stage of the questioning, this impressed Lynx, who would have asked how the card worked, rather than ordering the spy to tell them. It showed that Clive really had experience with interrogations.

"It's a Thark thing," the Vergallian panted, still eyeing Beowulf in fear. "You bring the captured agent, that's me,

157

to any Thark embassy, and present the swap card. They'll hold me until my side brings in your guy, then they let us both go. It's not a big deal, they do it all the time."

"What's in it for the Tharks?" Lynx asked, forgetting that she wasn't part of the interrogation scheme. The alien turned his head on the floor to face her, and he looked relieved to be talking to somebody other than the two ex-mercenaries.

"The Tharks sell the swap cards," the Vergallian explained. "It's sort of an insurance policy for undercover agents. They also sell ransom cards in war zones, but only the upper classes can afford them."

Joe tapped Beowulf on the side of his nose to get the dog's attention and pantomimed licking something. Beowulf grimaced, gave Joe a mournful look, and then dragged his rough tongue over the alien's face from the ear to the nose.

"Torture!" the Vergallian whimpered, turning away from Lynx. "What do you want from me? If I'm not in good condition, the Tharks won't make the trade."

"Tell us your orders," Joe growled. "Don't leave anything out."

Beowulf, who had turned his head away and licked himself a few times to get the taste of the Vergallian out of his mouth, turned back again, and allowed his tongue to loll over his lower teeth in an impressive display of pink muscle. The alien agent capitulated.

"I've been training for this assignment for two years," the face dancer groaned. "I spent most of that time living on your miserable planet, learning to speak this language that sounds like children's gibberish. I'm really an actor by training. I played human parts in some documentaries about your barbaric history. We originally planned to set up a private espionage agency, with me as the human owner, and my controller was going to feed me some juicy intelligence I could use to convince EarthCent to trust us. But just when we were getting ready to launch, you went and started your own stupid intelligence agency."

"Then you kidnapped Tom Curran and assumed his identity," Clive told him, having made good use of the alleged torture time to consult his tab and figure out who was missing.

"He was the right height and build," the Vergallian explained. "I can do faces, as long as the general shape is close. It was all very last-minute. I only got assigned the mission yesterday after we grabbed your man in our section. I was going to be your star agent."

"A mole," Lynx provided the technical term, having finished reading the twentieth century spy novels she was originally provided as training materials.

"I think he's telling the truth," Clive said to Joe, setting the older man up to play bad cop to his good cop.

"Maybe," Joe replied, absently scratching Beowulf behind the ears. "What do you say, boy?"

Beowulf went nose-to-nose with the supine Vergallian for the second time, staring down at the alien through unblinking eyes. The face dancer's features locked in a rictus of fear. The dog almost looked disappointed when he lifted up his massive head and gave Joe the nod. The would-be mole had passed the canine polygraph test.

"You two, get him on his feet," Clive ordered Lynx and the man who had asked the question about training for analysts. "Do you have any binders, Joe?"

"Got something better," Joe replied, assigning Beowulf another mission. "Duct tape, boy!" The dog gave Joe his best "You owe me big," look, before trotting off to retrieve a roll of one of Earth's most popular manufactured goods from the jumble of tools and supplies under the back of the ice harvester.

The Vergallian was too shaken to remain on his feet and sat back down on the floor, watching fearfully for the return of the giant dog. Convinced he wasn't going to make a sudden break for freedom, Lynx sidled up to Clive and whispered, "How about his implants? He's seen us all, and the facility, too."

Clive nodded and concentrated for a moment, his eyes straight ahead, but Lynx could see his lips moving slightly, typical for humans who hadn't learned to subvoc at an early enough age. After his lips stopped moving, he was still for a longer period, listening. When the subvoced conversation was completed, he addressed the trainees.

"Everybody take ten and relax," Clive said. "We're confirming the mole's story with the Tharks. If it checks out, Joe and Lynx will escort him to the Thark embassy for the exchange. I'm sure Beowulf would enjoy the exercise as well."

"Hear that, boy?" Joe asked the dog, when Beowulf arrived back with a roll of silver duct tape in his mouth. "We're going for a W - A - L - K." As he peeled off a two-foot-long strip of tape, the Vergallian hopefully extended his arms before him, wrists crossed. Beowulf gave a growl, and the alien immediately turned around, offering his wrists crossed behind his back instead. Joe wrapped the tape around and then added a second strip. In the meantime, Clive took Lynx aside for a private talk.

"Good thinking about the implant. We're going to have to look into technology for dealing with implant memories of spies in the future," Clive said. "Blythe isn't worried about it in this case. For the Vergallian to show up here this morning means they knew we were setting up camp, and even though we had the Drazens sweep the place for bugs, they probably watched the corridor and got everybody's faces recorded already."

"That makes sense," Lynx admitted. "How come you picked me to go with Joe and the dog to the Thark embassy?"

"We're grooming you," Clive told her bluntly. "Even the most horizontal organization needs to have somebody in charge. Blythe and I intend to do a lot of traveling and we can't always come running to deal with every issue. At the moment, you and Thomas are numbers three and four on our depth chart."

"I've never been groomed for anything before," Lynx said with a happy grin. "It may take me a while to get used to it. And sorry about interrupting your interrogation. You guys are really good at it."

"Lots of aliens end up using human mercenaries as auxiliary police departments on their outposts. Both Joe and I have a few years of experience with it."

"Is that because mercenaries are outsiders, so there's less politics?" Lynx conjectured.

"It's because mercenaries are cheap temporary help without benefits," Clive replied with a laugh. "Now, keep a hand on the Vergallian's elbow while you're walking him, and he'll assume that you know what you're doing. And don't worry. Between Joe and the dog, there won't be any surprises."

"Ready to go, boy?" Joe asked the dog, as Lynx came up and took a hold of the alien's elbow.

Beowulf stretched and nodded, thinking, the sooner we leave, the sooner we'll get back. Back from the W - A - L - K. After which you owe me a B - E - E - R.

Joe held up his right hand with his index and forefinger pressed together, scout's honor. He wasn't a telepath, but it wasn't hard to guess what the dog was thinking, and Beowulf always smiled with his eyes when he spelled "beer."

Fifteen

"You're doing a great job, Aisha," Kelly reassured her intern in her best professional tone. The ambassador was making her scheduled monthly visit to the office while taking Samuel out for a stroll, and praising the girl at the embassy was a different thing than encouraging her at home. "I've asked Donna to put in for EarthCent approval to let you keep the temporary acting junior consul job permanently."

"Thank you," Aisha responded, even as she struggled to interpret the new modifier to her compound title. "But can somebody be permanently temporary?"

"Yes, actually, though that's not what I meant," Kelly answered. "I requested that your internship be upgraded to an acting junior consul slot, but not permanently, since that would imply you couldn't be promoted again. And congratulations, that's a year faster than I made it."

"Is there a pay cut?" Aisha inquired cautiously, having learned that nothing involving EarthCent promotions was as simple as it seemed.

"Not since InstaSitter started sponsoring the embassy," Kelly told her. "I have to hand it to Blythe, she doesn't skimp on salary. Anything I need to catch up on?"

"Are you serious?" Aisha demanded. "For the last two weeks, every time I tried to bring up work, you told me to wait until you visited the office. I'm beginning to feel guilty that I don't push Paul harder to move out of Mac's Bones and give you some privacy."

"That's silly," Kelly told her. "You know we have plenty of room, and Joe and I are the ones who should feel guilty, with all of the free babysitting you do for us. Speaking of which, Samuel should be getting hungry in about twenty minutes, so let's get started."

The ambassador took the bassinet holding her four-month-old son from the display desk and put it on the floor. Then she thought better of it, moved the bassinet to the chair, and rolled the chair out of the way.

"Well, you know that we're completely sold out for booth spaces," Aisha began her recitation. "And when I opened a reservations list for a potential show next year, all of the same vendors signed up immediately. It makes you wonder how they sold their spy stuff until now."

"Probably with some difficulty, or they wouldn't be so enthusiastic about the show," Kelly replied. "Any real surprises, or is it pretty much the usual suspects?"

"Ever hear of the Cherts?" Aisha asked the ambassador.

"No, they must not have a presence on the station, or maybe they aren't nitrogen/oxygen breathers," Kelly guessed. "When it comes down to it, we don't mix much with the non-humanoid types who can't get by on nose filters. It's hard to do diplomacy in person when one of the parties is wearing a full environmental suit."

"I took the Chert who came in for human at first, but the yellow eyes and teeth were a bit of a giveaway," Aisha replied. "It turns out they have most of the deck above this one, and Libby says that there are about two million of them on the station."

"How come we never met?" Kelly asked.

"According to Srizzle, that's as close as I can come to pronouncing his name, they were just waiting for the right business opportunity," Aisha explained. "I guess they aren't very social, and they're experts in stealth technology, so we don't see them unless they want to be seen. They were almost tempted out of their voluntary seclusion a few years ago when InstaSitter launched, but in the end, they worried it would interfere with their balance of trade."

"A little babysitting would have impacted their bottom line?" Kelly said in amazement. "I know InstaSitter isn't exactly cheap, but still, it's just babysitting."

"Srizzle explained that too. Since they currently don't do any business with the other station species, being hidden and all, they worried about their exchange rate with the Stryx cred. But now they hope they can sell enough counter-surveillance equipment to come out of hiding. He seemed very nice."

"Alright, a race of hidden aliens living right above our heads, that's pretty impressive. Anything else I need to know?"

"A group called the Artificial Intelligence Knights took four folds. They're selling intelligence from all over the galaxy. I asked Libby about them, and she said that while the Stryx know of their existence, they are actually a very secretive group and they mainly operate outside of Stryx space. One of their robots stopped by the office to barter information in lieu of the vendor fee, but I told him I wasn't authorized."

"Artificial Intelligence Knights," Kelly mused, trying out the acronym. "AIK. Ache? Sounds like they're coming out of the woodwork for this one. Anything else?"

"I've been meaning to ask you why the Empire Convention Center hall we rented is the Nebulae room, rather than Nebula. I mean, it's the plural, right? It's never the Galaxies room or the Black Holes room."

"Do they actually have a Black Hole room?"

"Yes. I stuck my head in the door when I went over to look at the available options and I won't do that again," Aisha replied ruefully. "I tried to ask the Dollnick secretary in charge of the room bookings about the name, but she said that information was on a need-to-know basis. I swear this spy show is making everybody crazy."

"It's good to be curious, Aisha, but you have to prioritize," Kelly cautioned her intern. "We already rented the Nebulae room once. The name was the same then and the show was a great success, so I'd be more concerned if it suddenly changed."

"Knock, Knock," Donna said as she entered the room. "You know that you have a meeting here with Bork in a half an hour, right?"

Kelly nodded her head in the affirmative. She was looking forward to meeting her friend after seeing the Drazen ambassador so infrequently while on maternity leave. At first she was a little offended that he didn't come by Mac's Bones to fuss over the baby. Then Tinka explained that in Drazen culture, males were persona non grata around babies until the mother and child had a chance to Sh'krint, a word the implant failed to translate, but which the Drazen girl related to the human concept of bonding.

"He's bringing another Drazen diplomat, their cultural attaché for the entire station network," Donna added significantly. Cultural attaché? A little bell in Kelly's head

166

dinged, and it wasn't her implant announcing that her mother was calling long distance.

"Well, I'm sure anybody with an interest in human culture on the stations would love to meet the founders of InstaSitter," Kelly replied slowly. "Is Blythe around?"

"She and Clive showed up at breakfast this morning," Donna answered. "I'll just ping her and see if she's free."

Aisha watched their faces closely, observing that the two older women's speech had subtly changed over the last couple sentences, and she guessed that something related to spying was afoot.

"Speaking of Drazens, I haven't seen the office cleaners in a while," Aisha ventured.

"We only scheduled that service once," Donna answered. "We're hoping to give the work to a human cleaning service, as long as they can buy the appropriate supplies."

"Oh, that reminds me!" Aisha exclaimed, rising from the desk. Despite her involvement in the trade show, she was still doing her best to know as little about what was going on with the new intelligence agency as possible. "If you don't need me for an hour or so, I haven't shopped for dinner yet, and all the fresh vegetables will be gone soon."

"Go, go," Kelly replied, and watched her softhearted daughter-in-law vanish out the door. "I'm going to feed the baby, Donna. If Blythe can't make it, can you send somebody to tear Joe away from whatever he's doing?"

"Will do," Donna replied with a wink, and keyed the door shut as she passed into the outer office.

Left alone, Kelly picked up the baby, who was just starting to fuss, and began to nurse. After relaxing for a few minutes, something occurred to her, and she asked, "Libby?"

"Welcome back to your office, Kelly. How can I help you," answered the Stryx librarian's familiar voice.

"What's the most valuable commodity in the galaxy?"

"In the entire galaxy, or just in the parts connected by our tunnel network?" Libby responded.

"The tunnel network parts."

"There are several ways of looking at it," Libby replied, either pondering the question or trying to decide how much she should tell Kelly.

"I'm not thinking about the ice market, or food and energy, so maybe commodity is the wrong word." Kelly reflected for a moment and tried to clarify her query. "I'm thinking more about finished goods, the products the different species specialize in, where there are unique ingredients, special techniques, secret formulas, that sort of thing."

"Are you interested in individual items, like General Tso's Chicken, or broad categories, like take-out food?"

"The broadest," Kelly replied, wondering why Libby had chosen the particular example she did. "Like take-out food or clothing."

"Entertainment," Libby answered with a single word.

"That's what I thought!" Kelly exclaimed. "I don't ever hear about entertainment from my contacts on the station because none of them are in the business. But all the time I've been spending reading, listening to music and watching holo entertainment while I'm on leave got me wondering about it. I even tried a couple of alien romances in translation, but they read more like history or business books than like novels. Dring once told me that's because human relationships are so irrational, and we expect plots to be even more exaggerated in our stories and plays. But I wondered whether the artistic output of other species finds a market beyond their native audience."

"I don't think I'll be spoiling anybody's business if I told you that most species purposefully target their entertainment productions to meet the largest possible market," Libby replied. "Critics complain that over millions of years, it's led to homogenization of galactic cultures, and that's why the documentaries on new species are so popular."

"Because the stories are new," Kelly speculated.

"Exactly," Libby replied. "Even if you ignored books and games, the market for immersive productions from different species is the largest cash-flow item on the Stryx cred report that we issue once a cycle."

"Just out of curiosity, can you tell me what the biggest product is outside of Stryx space?"

"Weapons," Libby replied sadly. "Oops, you have visitors in the outer office. Time to burp the baby."

Kelly rose hastily, straightened her clothes, and walked to the door. She swiped the door lock and stepped through the opening just as Donna was showing Bork and an older Drazen to seats.

"I hope we didn't interrupt you," Bork said, looking slightly embarrassed in the presence of a woman carrying a baby. "Donna was just telling us that you haven't had our cleaning friends back recently."

"I'm afraid so," Kelly admitted. "I was only expecting a, uh, social visit. Do you think we should head somewhere else?"

"No, no," Bork's companion spoke up jovially. "I am Cultural Attaché Herl, though the women call me whatever they want."

"I've heard that somewhere before," Kelly replied with a smile, extending her free hand to shake with Herl. "Please, come in. Bork, can you bring an extra chair?"

"I can bring two extra chairs," Bork replied, and proceeded to lift one in each hand. He gave a friendly wave to Donna with his tentacle as he followed Herl and Kelly into the inner office.

Bork placed the two chairs in front of Kelly's display desk and sat down in one, but Herl remained on his feet, displaying a pent-up energy that made Kelly wonder if he was going to burst into dance. He smiled at her and ostentatiously scratched behind his back with his left hand, which struck her as odd, since Drazens usually used their tentacle to deal with itches it could reach. Then she noticed that one of the buttons on the cuff of his shirtsleeve was blinking red.

Herl did a slow circuit of her office, keeping up a knowledgeable patter about the human art that she had hung on the walls, which was all the more impressive for the fact that she hadn't hung anything. He spent almost a minute admiring a non-existent vase in the corner, by the end of which time, Kelly had to blink to assure herself that it wasn't really there. Finally, he examined the baby's bassinet and made the appropriate cooing noises for Samuel, who favored him with a smile.

"Did you see that?" Kelly asked, momentarily forgetting about the blinking red button. "That's the first time he's smiled for a stranger."

"I'm honored," Herl replied sincerely, taking his seat. "I have to admit, there's so much splendid art in this room that I don't think I could talk about boring galactic business matters and pretend that it's just not there."

"I understand," Kelly replied, wondering how to convey the message to Blythe and Clive when they arrived. Then again, the two of them would likely recognize the situation right off, without the need for an elaborate play. "Is this your first time on Union Station?"

"First time in a while," Herl admitted. "Stations aren't usually such interesting places for men in my profession. When I was new in my post, I thought that Stryx stations were the ideal place to meet aliens for cultural exchanges, but it turns out that the experience is quite diluted compared to that of encountering the different species on their home turf."

"I never thought of it that way," Kelly admitted. "I suppose that's because everything about the other species is so new to humans, and there are so many of you. We're still in the survey stage, rather than trying to dig deeply into what makes you all tick."

"What makes us tick!" Bork exclaimed. "Excellent analogy. Didn't I tell you she has a gift for language, Herl."

Kelly didn't hear the cultural attaché's response if he made one, because Donna took the same moment to inform the ambassador over her implant that Blythe and Clive had arrived. To her surprise, Blythe entered the room with Tinka, and Clive followed behind carrying the last two guest chairs from the outer office. Kelly quickly made the introductions between all parties, who judging from their reactions, seemed to know each other already by reputation. Herl held up his wrist with the blinking red light, causing Tinka's eyes to narrow. Clive shrugged and Blythe didn't react at all.

"How generous of you to take time out of your busy day to talk with us about human culture on the station network," Herl declared. "Your InstaSitter business is the envy of many a Drazen businessman. It's funny how we older species fall into the habit of thinking that all of the good ideas have already been taken, and then a new race comes along and proves us wrong."

"We couldn't have done it without the Stryx infrastructure," Blythe replied graciously. "Our build-out would have been much slower, and I doubt we could have coped with better financed competition from the older species. It's not like we could keep it a secret after we started advertising."

"Yes, it's interesting what one can learn through advertisements," Herl concurred. "But there is so much media, so many ads. It would be quite expensive for a business to monitor all of them alone."

"Yes, it's hard to do anything alone," Blythe acknowledged carefully. "Even with my sister and the Stryx, it wasn't long before we found ourselves relying on Tinka for help with daily operations."

"I heard from Bork that you made young Tinka a stakeholder in your business," Herl responded. "I was very impressed that humans were already teaming with other species on the equity level. Some aliens have never come that far along."

"We're great believers in team building," Clive said, taking his wife's hand as he spoke. "We're both convinced that good communications and trust are the secret to success in work and in life. Right, Honey?"

"Of course, and our management team has established those already with Tinka," Blythe observed.

"That makes perfect sense," Herl replied, with a sidelong look at the young Drazen woman. "You know, it's been a number of years since I played a sport myself, but I've always been struck by how much difference a leader can make, especially on a young team."

"We have so much to learn about Drazen culture and I'm not very familiar with your sports," Clive responded cautiously. "I can tell you that for humans, the coach is viewed as such a critical position that our old nation states often hired coaches from competing countries, even for the teams that represented their nation."

"Interesting analogy," Herl said. "In a sense, your people were much better prepared to encounter the array of species which populate our galaxy than those races who have achieved peace and uniformity before venturing out to the stars."

"I'm sure you're right, but sometimes I think humans are too adaptable," Blythe replied, her eyes closed in concentration. "It's only been a few generations since Earth was opened, and there are still plenty of elderly people who remember the old world, but institutions that lose continuity lose knowledge as well. I was talking to our ambassador just the other day about the similarities between the interstellar ice harvesting treaty and the ocean treaties that established fishing quotas for nations on Earth. Of course, the need for regulation disappeared when the majority of the human population emigrated, but if there was a need to protect the oceans today, we'd have to rebuild that institutional knowledge from scratch."

Kelly pressed her hands to her temples, trying to keep up with the coded negotiations taking place inside of the conversation about team spirit and fishing. It was all a bit much for somebody who was officially still on maternity leave, but everybody else seemed happy with the progress, so she held her peace and wondered where Blythe had really learned about fishing treaties. It was the first time Kelly had ever heard anything on the subject.

"It's wise of you to recognize the importance of institutional knowledge," Herl replied. "I understand that EarthCent is planning to establish its own program for cultural exchanges, and as the senior cultural attaché of the Drazen diplomatic service, I can assure you of our full support in getting started. In return, I hope Ambassador McAllister will put me at the top of her guest list any time she throws an embassy party."

"That goes without saying," Kelly said, after she realized the long pause in the negotiations meant that everybody was waiting for her to speak. In for a penny, in for a pound. "I'm sure you'll be at the top of the list for all EarthCent embassy parties."

Bork positively beamed at Kelly, giving her an affirmative nod, and Herl smiled broadly. Blythe and Clive relaxed in their chairs, and Tinka looked pleased as well.

"Thank you for allowing me to view your private art collection, Ambassador, and I'm sure we'll be seeing each other at your trade show," Herl declared, rising to his feet. "It was very nice to meet you also, Mr. and Mrs. Oxford, Tinka. I didn't want to bore the ambassadors with my questions about the details of your babysitting business, but perhaps I can convince the three of you to return to my temporary office at the Drazen embassy and we can discuss all of the practical issues. I'm very interested in hearing about that old ship you salvaged as well."

"We'd be happy to do that," Clive replied. "Thank you for the introduction, Ambassadors," he continued, nodding to both Bork and Kelly. "I'll have these chairs straightened out in a moment."

The room emptied rapidly and Kelly was left alone with Samuel, who was sound asleep. Donna entered the office looking amused and headed right over to the baby.

"Did you get her to hold him?" she asked, leaving Kelly to figure out she meant Blythe and Samuel.

"No," Kelly responded. "They talked about sports and fishing for a few minutes and then they left in a hurry. I'm going to take Sammy and head home."

"Enjoy the rest of your maternity leave," Donna said. "If you need a sitter, just call me."

Sixteen

"So, tomorrow is the big day," Joe said, leaning back from the table with a satisfied sigh. He liked his own barbeque, and Kelly's cooking wasn't bad, but Aisha was on the professional level when she cooked Indian food. "You kids might want to visit some of the clubs around the convention center hotel district to see what you're going to be up against."

"Are you assigning that as a training mission?" Lynx asked, simultaneously tapping Thomas on the shoulder to get his attention.

"I'm number five on the chart," Joe reminded her. "How can I assign you anything?"

"It sounds like a good idea to me," Thomas said. "It feels like we haven't done anything constructive since the trip to Seventy. Besides, I've been promising Chance we'd take her out one night and let her show off her new fuel cell."

"Why didn't you suggest it to the trainees?" Lynx asked Joe. "They've all been working hard, and a chance to combine a little work and recreation is always a good idea."

"Things can go downhill in a hurry when aliens and alcohol are involved," Joe explained. "Besides, the trainees have to be here first thing in the morning for a covert communications class conducted by the Drazen expert Herl loaned us. I'm looking forward to that one myself."

"I still think Thomas and I should take it as well," Lynx complained.

"Hey, I don't make the rules," Joe replied with a shrug. "Clive and Blythe have been spending a lot of time with Herl, and apparently he convinced them that it's important for morale and the command structure not to let the new recruits get too familiar with their superiors. If we had let you keep training with them, they would have ended up thinking of you as just another agent as opposed to the crown princess."

"Is Lynx royalty and nobody told me?" Kelly asked, returning to the table after checking on the baby.

"Sorry, it's all those worlds with monarchies I served on," Joe said. "I keep on thinking of Clive and Blythe as the king and queen, which makes these two the crown prince and princess."

"You told me I was the princess," Dorothy piped up. "And you said Sammy is the little prince!"

"Of course I did, princess," Joe replied, rising to his feet and lifting his daughter out of her chair. "We were talking about a different kingdom for grown-ups."

"Oh, then you can be a princess too," Dorothy told Lynx graciously.

"Uh, thanks, I guess," Lynx replied, having lost track of the royal succession by this point. "Is EarthCent doing an official welcome thing at any of these bars?"

"Oh, I knew I forgot to tell you something," Kelly exclaimed. "Donna rented out a place called Casablanca for the night, apparently it's the biggest human-themed bar in that area. She's going to set up a table and start handing out conference badges for the preregistered attendees so they won't have to wait in line tomorrow. It was a last-second thing Stanley suggested to reduce the crush in the morning, and Chastity will be there tonight to help as well."

"So I guess we'll make the Casablanca our first stop," Lynx replied. "All set, partner?

"Yes, and thank you for dinner," Thomas said politely as he rose from the table. "I'm sorry about not eating anything, but it all looked delicious."

"I understand," Aisha said, blushing lightly. She hadn't encountered any artificial persons on Earth, and not that many since arriving on Union Station, so she was still a little uncomfortable socializing with an AI that was indistinguishable from a human. "Maybe I'll see you at the Casablanca later, if Paul wants to go out."

The two EarthCent Intelligence agents exited Mac's Bones and walked to the nearest lift tube. When the door slid shut, they spoke simultaneously, Thomas saying, "Casablanca," and Lynx saying, "Prudence." The lift, intelligently, remained stationary.

"Need something back at the ship?" Thomas asked.

"I just didn't want to get there too early," Lynx replied. "I love eating with Joe and his family, but they're kind of on kiddy time, if you haven't noticed."

"Not really, but time was never my strong suit. Besides, I already pinged Chance and she's on her way to meet us."

"Casablanca," Lynx commanded, and the lift capsule accelerated smoothly. In less than a minute, the door opened on a cacophony of blaring musical styles from dozens of different species. The sounds emanated from the fronts of the open café-style bars that dominated the corridor. Lynx had been to her share of rowdy bar districts on stations and trading outposts around Stryx space, but the sheer gaudiness of the scene took her breath away.

"I hope there's a dance floor in the Casablanca," Thomas shouted over the noise. He led Lynx off to the left, where he had spotted the name 'Casablanca' spelled out in red neon letters, with a brace of green neon palm trees hanging over them.

"I hope there's an active acoustic filter," Lynx shouted back. "Why is it so crazy here?"

"Salesmen," Thomas asserted loudly. "I worked at the Empire as a busboy and a runner back before I got the InstaSitter job. Normally I can tell the different species apart by their behavioral characteristics before processing the visual data. But with salesmen, it's faster to look for visual cues, like a tentacle, the number of fingers or the color of the skin."

"You mean they all act the same way?" Lynx shouted back as they pushed through a crowd of tipsy Frunge and into the Casablanca, where the noise level instantly dropped off as if they had passed through an invisible wall. It was replaced by the sound of a live quintet: piano, two violins, a guitar and a bass, along with the tinkle of ice in liquor-filled tumblers against a background of subdued conversation.

"Pretty much," Thomas replied softly, lowering his voice to match the environment. They looked around the bar for Donna and Chastity, but apparently Lynx was right about arriving early. Thomas nudged Lynx and pointed to the bare back and prominent spine of a woman placing an order at the bar. "Hey, that woman is practically naked!"

"Chance," Lynx called, and the woman in the slinky dress turned from the bar, a bottle of vodka in one hand, and a small tray with three glasses and a bowl of peanuts in the other. The artificial person had her hair piled up, revealing a slender neck, along with perfect collar bones, and a skirt that was slit up the side almost to the level of the plunging back line. All cleaned up with a full charge, Chance featured a million-watt smile.

"Hi, guys," she called breezily, meeting them halfway across the room. "Thanks for inviting me out early, Thomas. I was beginning to go stir crazy waiting for the starting time."

"So you've really joined the firm?" Lynx asked cautiously.

"Yes, I have, but tonight is my first official assignment," Chance replied. "I had been hoping to pick up some extra cash working for InstaSitter, but Chastity said I failed the babysitter profile on every possible match point."

"That's amazing," Thomas remarked as he steered them to an open table. "I matched every point in the babysitting profile. Funny how AI works." He took the bottle and filled all three glasses.

"Skol!" Lynx toasted, lifting up her glass. Chance and Thomas quickly followed suit and tossed theirs back in one swallow, leaving Lynx behind with a half empty glass and a pessimistic outlook for the evening.

"You know, Clive showed me the organization chart for our agency, and I found out that I'm working for you guys," Chance continued with wide-eyed enthusiasm. "Isn't that great?"

"Sure," Lynx replied, with all of the team spirit she could muster. "But we only came at the last minute on Joe's suggestion to take a look around tonight. Did you say you were coming out later on a mission anyway?"

"I'm ready to start working any minute," Chance replied perkily, twisting her shoulders back and forth and smiling like the Cheshire cat. "I'm supposed to have a good time and keep my ears open, of course. You guys might think that I don't have any experience at this sort of thing, but I've worked the bars for a few businesses over the years."

After finishing her shot to keep from commenting that she wasn't at all surprised, the burn in her throat and stomach made Lynx wonder if they were feeding her grain alcohol. She excused herself and went to the bar to order a plain orange juice as a mixer. By the time she got back, the table was abandoned, and she worried for a moment that somebody had put the bag on her fellow agents. Then, a spotlight focused on the small dance floor, and there were Thomas and Chance in a classic pose. The band struck up an Argentinean tango, and they began to move counterclockwise in an intricate weave of motion.

Lynx stared in fascination as the dancers alternatively extended themselves in graceful lunges, one leg stretched far behind, and flowed into a spin move that included intricate patterns drawn mid-air by the lower leg and foot. But her jaw dropped when Chance threw a leg high in the air and brought it down over her partner's thigh, and then lifted her other leg off the ground while Thomas supported her weight, her knee reaching his shoulder and her toe pointed in the air well above his head. The slit in her dress exposed both of her legs to the waist, revealing her lacy black panties. The crowd burst into applause, Lynx joining them.

Three minutes later, the dancers were back at the table, Thomas his usual cool and debonair self, Chance blushing and panting, despite the fact that she had no lungs and a full charge. Lynx was beginning to see how the artificial person might prove an effective Mata Hari, one of the more interesting personages described in the so-called training materials. And as Thomas poured a glass for his tango partner, Lynx detected something she never would have expected to see, a tremor in his hand.

"That was incredible!" declared a voice over Lynx's head. She turned in her chair to see Chastity had arrived, along with Tinka and Donna. "Can you teach me?" the girl asked Thomas.

Thomas gave Chance a questioning look, to which she responded with a demure smile and a little hand motion. Lynx's partner bounded to his feet and led Chastity to the dance floor, where the band left off the instrumental number they were playing and struck up another tango.

"She just finished telling me how good she was at alphabetizing alien names," Donna complained as she watched her daughter go. "Ah, there's our reserved table. I'd invite you girls to help, but it's probably better for your business if you aren't seen with me."

"Our business?" Lynx asked Chance, as the EarthCent embassy manager and Tinka begin setting up columns of preprogrammed show badges on the large table with a "Reserved for EarthCent" sign.

"Making friends and extracting information," Chance replied brightly. "I never would have guessed that Thomas was such a good dancer," she added, casting her eyes back to the dance floor where Chastity was apparently trying to poke holes in the artificial person's shoes with her heels. "He seemed rather stuffy up until now, you know?"

"Oh, he's a barrel of laughs once you get to know him," Lynx replied reflexively, wondering if this was really why Joe had suggested the outing. She reached for the bottle, telling herself she would have just a little dash in her orange juice, when a strange man settled into the chair that had been occupied by Thomas.

"If you're going to drink that swill, you may as well just hit your head on the wall until you get dizzy for all the pleasure it will bring you," the man declared in a strange accent. "Allow me to order a bottle of the good stuff." Without waiting for their response, he snapped his fingers in the air and pointed at the table. The barman, whose attention Lynx had struggled to attract just a few minutes earlier, immediately said something to a waitress and indicated their table.

"Did you invite this guy to sit down?" Lynx asked Chance, forgetting for a moment that the mission was to mingle.

"No, he's all yours," Chance replied, rising to her feet. Either she had misunderstood the sarcasm in Lynx's question or she had spotted a target of opportunity approaching the EarthCent table. Before Lynx could respond, the waitress arrived with a bottle of aged, single malt Scotch. Chance turned on her smile and intercepted a Vergallian male who was wearing a uniform that made him look like an admiral or an opera star.

"I'm Ronk," Lynx's new table companion said with a leer, pouring out two glasses of the expensive booze. She studied his face and noted that the man might be wearing some kind of makeup, but the lighting was too low to tell if it was cosmetics or a minor radiation burn. "How does a beautiful babe like you end up in a hole like this?"

"I thought it was rather nice, until now," Lynx replied pointedly. Then she reminded herself of the mission and accepted the glass he was offering. It smelled heavenly, so she took a little sip and immediately started feeling better. "So what species are you, Ronk?"

"Drazen born and bred," the man admitted, throwing back the amber liquid in one go, and without the respect it deserved, Lynx thought. He looked at her in exasperation and added, "Were you planning on letting that Scotch evaporate and inhaling the fumes? Come on, live a little."

Lynx stared back at the Drazen, dumbfounded by his approach to tippling, then shrugged and tossed off the Scotch. It was his money, and she figured she may as well have a snort or two of the good stuff before he figured out she wasn't his type and moved on with his bottle. He immediately poured her a fresh one.

"Yeah, we Drazens really like you human women," he continued, draining a second glass and looking at her expectantly. When Lynx failed to respond by dissolving into blushes or bending her elbow, he paused to reassess the situation. She noticed for the first time that his tentacle was out and hanging limply, and she thought he must be pretty drunk already not to be discomfited by the way it was crushed between his shoulder and the chair.

"Are you on the station for the EarthCent show?" she asked, primarily because she wasn't interested in hearing whatever lame line he might come up with if left to make conversation on his own.

"Vendor, I'm working a booth," he responded. "Heard that you humans are finally getting in the game, and I got me an expense account, so I thought, why not make nice and get a jump on the show?"

"I only heard about the show through friends," Lynx ventured cautiously, sipping at her new drink. "I'm an independent trader myself."

"Of course you are," Ronk replied with an exaggerated wink. He even threw in the archaic 'okay' sign she had seen only in historical dramas, making a circle with his thumb and forefinger and holding the other three fingers out.

"Wow," Lynx said out loud, struck by the incredible cheesiness of the guy. If he had been from any other species, she could have tried to pump him for information, but Blythe and Clive had concluded a cooperation pact with the Drazens, making them allies. She wondered why he was wasting time on her, and what it was about him that struck her as a little off.

"So tell me about the trading business," her companion said, topping off her glass even though she'd barely downed a third of the contents. "I do a lot of traveling myself, so I'm always interested in hearing about the latest conditions here and there. Been anywhere interesting lately?"

"Oh, round and about," she started to reply, but then she had a sudden urge to shock the complacent look off of his unnaturally colored face. "To tell you the truth, I had to dump a cargo of contraband on my last trip. Turned out the stuff was banned in Stryx space."

"Really?" He leaned forward, and Lynx got the impression that his face had become tinged with purple. "Just stuff you were bringing in for yourself, or on the job?"

"What job? I'm an independent," she repeated, causing the expert in human behavior to flash another 'okay' sign. Lynx froze for a moment as she finally picked up on what was bothering her. Didn't Drazens have six fingers? She tried to distract him by leaning forward herself while looking surreptitiously at his other hand to see if he had lost a finger in an accident. Nope, and furthermore, when she looked up he was staring in her eyes, when a real Drazen would have been looking down her dress.

185

Steeling herself, she smiled and leaned even closer, so their noses were almost touching. Then she reached around him with her free arm as if to pull his head in for a kiss. Instead, she grabbed his tentacle and sat back in her chair, hard. The rubberized prosthetic came away in her hand and she slapped it down on the table between them. The faux Drazen yelped and began to look very annoyed.

"You pulled off a layer of skin with the glue," he accused her. "One spy to another, what gave me away?"

Lynx tossed back her Scotch to counter her surging adrenaline and extended the empty glass. "One spy to another, it'll cost you."

He grudgingly refilled her glass, but she could tell by the way he pulled the bottle back afterwards that the party was over. She looked again at his hands, and this time, she noticed that the palm of his drinking hand was too red. A glimpse of his glass showed that some make-up had rubbed off on it, so the Scotch was probably a solvent.

"You're Horten, right?" she guessed. They were pretty standard humanoids other than their inability to control the color of their skin, which shifted with their emotions. It was the best explanation for all of the make-up.

"No law against it, and I am working the booth, so I wonder who's the bigger liar between the two of us," he shot back. "Now what tipped you off?"

"Digits," she replied, making a show of counting from her thumb to her pinkie "You don't have enough of them."

The glasses bounced in the air as he slammed his fist on the table. "I knew I forgot something when I left the hotel room. I just couldn't put my finger on it."

"Is that an idiom in Horten, or was my translation implant making a joke?" Lynx asked.

186

"No more Scotch for you," the Horten declared. He picked up his prosthetic and the bottle and stalked away. Lynx sat back with relief as Thomas and Chastity returned.

"Did you see me?" Chastity asked breathlessly. "I was beginning to get it. Thomas promised to give me lessons while he's on the station."

"Where's Chance?" Thomas asked, slowly surveying the room.

"When some Horten impersonating a Drazen sat down, she set off after a Vergallian," Lynx replied.

"Damn Vergallians," Thomas growled, sounding very much like Joe.

"How can a Horten impersonate a Drazen?" Chastity asked. "Drazens have a tentacle and six fingers, and Hortens change color if you blow on them."

"He had a fake tentacle, he took it with him," Lynx explained. "Wait, when did you ever blow on a Horten?"

"Babysitting," Chastity replied, looking enviously at Lynx's glass. "Is that top shelf?"

"Take it." Lynx pushed the Scotch across the table. "I'm half in the bag already and we haven't been here an hour. This job is hard."

Four hours later, Donna, Chastity and Tinka packed up the preprogrammed badges that hadn't been claimed. After the tentacle incident, Lynx had inserted her other half into the bag, so Chastity shook her awake and dragged her home to sleep in Blythe's old room.

Thomas and Chance returned to the dance floor, doing a slow hug-and-sway that was completely at odds with the music. Since the artificial people were the only sober sentients left in the place, it was probably the band that was out of sync.

187

Seventeen

"Well, look what the cat dragged in," Donna greeted Lynx, adding a sympathetic smile. The embassy manager and Aisha were manning the registration desk in the roped off area of the convention center lobby. "It's never a good idea to be early on the first day of these things in any case. The vendors are all hung over and it was a madhouse earlier."

"Are Blythe and Clive around somewhere?" Lynx croaked, her voice sounding like she'd spent the previous evening gargling whiskey, which wasn't far from the truth. At least she had remembered to bring her antique camera, with the express intent of using up the roll so she could send the film out for development.

"Yes, they have a booth set up just inside," Donna replied. "You can't miss it."

Lynx began to shoulder her way past the Gem saleswomen who formed a cordon across the entrance. The Gem were making the best of their assigned space in the overflow area by intercepting visitors before they got inside the Nebulae room. Lynx stumbled to a halt when she was blocked by a clone balancing a round tray on her fingertips. The tray held dozens of small plastic tumblers filled with a chalky grey fluid.

"Cures hangovers," the Gem declared after one quick look at the human. Lynx was hooked.

"Is it safe for human consumption?" she grunted, annoyed with herself for talking to a clone, but desperate to get rid of the dull pounding in her temples.

"Absolutely," the middle-aged woman assured her with a cold smile. "Compliments of Gem Internal Security."

Lynx shuddered, took a cup from the tray, and poured the gritty mixture down her throat. She staggered for a moment as she felt her stomach and sinuses being invaded by a swarm of angry ants, but then the hangover vanished like somebody had thrown a switch.

"That's amazing!" Lynx said in astonishment, replacing the tumbler on the tray. "You should sell this stuff around the galaxy. You'd make a fortune and everybody would love you, or at least, they might not despise you as much."

"Nanotracker is far too expensive to use as an everyday hangover cure," the Gem told her. "And keep the cup, the number on the bottom identifies the transmitter. You can map your movements on the big screen there when you come out."

The Gem pointed, indicating a giant display that Lynx had assumed was the EarthCent floor plan for visitors. Now she saw that in addition to showing all of the vendor booths, it was full of slowly moving avatars of different species, each accompanied by a little Gem logo. While she watched, a Dollnick exited the show and used the holo controller to select the four-armed avatar that stood right in front of the display. A detailed itinerary of the Dollnick's movements at the show appeared, along with times spent at various booths, total distance traveled, and biometric data about his bodily functions.

"You implanted a bug in me?" Lynx asked in shock.

"Nanotracker is more than a bug, it's the latest in full monitoring technology," the Gem recited. "The nanobots self-assemble into a short-range transmitter within two minutes of ingestion, and as you're now aware, they're also programmed to cure hangovers and indigestion. As a nontoxic, temporary means of tracking biologicals, Nanotracker is approved for use in Stryx space, as long as the subject ingests the drink voluntarily."

Lynx raised a hand to her mouth like she was going to barf, but her stomach, like her head, felt wonderful. Instead of making a fuss, she grumbled, "How temporary?"

"Nanotracker transits the digestive system in accordance with the natural rhythms of the biological," the Gem saleswoman continued with her pitch. "Eating acidic foods may shorten the life of the transmitter, as will strong magnetic fields. Of course, we also offer a Nanosolvent product that will destroy any and all nano-implants within minutes of ingestion, though some species complain about a sudden laxative effect. Nanotracker is available in quantities as small as one hundred doses, and you can select from any number of off-the-shelf receiver products. Don't forget to check your visit data on the way out," the Gem concluded breezily, before turning away from Lynx to block a bleary eyed Grenouthian. "Hello, bunny. Hangover?"

Lynx picked her way through the remaining Gem saleswomen and walked gingerly through the doors of the Nebulae room, rubbing her stomach. She couldn't help wondering if she had ever been Nanotracked before without even knowing it. Alien tech was so far in advance of Earth's that humans often didn't realize it was there until somebody pointed it out. It made her wonder what

Blythe and Clive could possibly be offering at the show to justify setting up a table. Then she saw the sign.

EarthCent Intelligence - Double agents wanted

"Hey, Lynx," Blythe called. "Come on over and we'll tell you about the good booths. Clive and I have been taking turns going through the show."

"What's going on?" Lynx whispered loudly as she approached her boss. "I thought we were supposed to be a secret agency."

"We talked it over with Kelly and realized it's way too late to stuff that cat back into the bag, so we may as well take advantage of it," Blythe replied cheerfully. "You, me, Thomas, Clive, our covers were blown by the surveillance the other species were running on EarthCent communications before we even got started. But what difference does it really make? Some of the aliens may run facial recognition screenings at customs on their home worlds or colonies, but it's not like the four of us will be going on undercover missions."

"Anyway, the Gem bugged me," Lynx confessed, figuring it was best to just get it over with.

"The Gem bug everybody," Blythe replied. "That's why they're out front."

"No, I mean they put a bug on me, or in me, with nanobots," Lynx explained.

"I heard they were doing that, but I thought you had to volunteer," Clive said, implying that he was surprised she had made that choice. "We got here early so they weren't set up yet, but I was thinking of trying it. Libby says that it's safe."

"Well, you don't need to now, I'll give you a full report," Lynx replied, feeling better about getting tricked by the clones. "So are you recruiting any double agents with the subtle approach?"

"We're getting a lot of bites," Blythe assured her. "Kelly talked to her Shuk contacts for us, and we were able to get these buttons made up before we opened this morning. They display in over a hundred languages."

"I'm a double agent for the humans," Lynx read aloud from an English version of the button. "Do aliens really wear these?"

"They're free," Blythe pointed out. "You could give away T-shirts printed with, 'Dump me in the vacuum,' and the attendees would snap them up."

"Can I take a look at your picture gadget?" Clive asked.

"It's a camera, a 35mm single reflex," Lynx said, handing it across the table to the head of EarthCent Intelligence. "There must be tens of millions of these kicking around people's attics back on Earth. They're just too nice to throw away."

"This is something," Clive said in admiration as he worked the adjustment rings on the lens. Then he looked through the viewer. "Hey, I can't see anything."

"You have to remove the lens cap," she told him. "Here, try now."

"Nice," he replied, focusing on a cluster of aliens on a raised stage at the center of the hall. "How do I make it work?"

"You start by manually focusing through the view finder, but I'd have to give you a lesson on getting the exposure right," Lynx replied. "I'll show you later if you want, but a room like this without a flash is a tough place to start learning."

"Fair enough," Clive replied, handing the camera back. "So we'll make you the official camera person for the day. Your mission is to document the trade show for our archives."

"But all you have to do is look at something and save the image on your implant," Lynx pointed out.

"Clive is just trying to keep your morale up," Blythe told her. "He's been reading about organizational leadership."

"I understand," Lynx replied, not really understanding, but ready to move on. "Any recommendations for must-see booths?

"It's a good thing the show is scheduled for three days because it's all interesting," Clive answered honestly. "Some of these species have been spying on each other for millions of years, and the countermeasures are even more amazing than the actual information-gathering devices. Make sure you don't miss the Cherts, they have the space between the Hortens and Dollnicks. And take one of these 'EarthCent Spy' bags for the freebies."

"Got it," Lynx acknowledged, moving out of the way to let a group of Verlocks step up and claim their double agent buttons. She spent a few seconds adjusting the aperture and exposure time to compensate for the artificial lighting and took a picture of the booth fronts along the aisle. Her hands were steady as a rock, thanks to the Gem nanobots.

After a long discussion with a Horten salesman about the intelligence value of their galactic news clipping service, Lynx wandered past an empty space where the vendors were either late or had folded up their tables and left early. She was about to move on to see what the

Dollnicks were offering, when a voice out of nowhere said, "Psssst, over here."

Lynx looked at the space where her ears told her the sound had originated, but saw nothing. "Hello?" she ventured.

"I'm right here," the voice insisted, making Lynx suspect that some alien species had finally turned ventriloquism into a real art. For the sake of doing something, she held up the camera and took a picture of the empty space. At least it would remind her of the experience when she got the prints.

"What was that?" the voice asked curiously.

"It's an invisibility neutralizer," Lynx replied, frustrated at being forced to converse with thin air. "In another ten seconds, either you'll be fully visible or I'll disappear. One or the other."

The empty space seemed to shimmer, and then a crowded booth area snapped into focus, as if a curtain had been drawn from the scene. The voice she had been engaged with turned out to belong to an attractive humanoid male whose eyes and teeth were a bright yellow. There was a slick device that looked like a miniature energy beam turret mounted on his shoulder, and he wore an "I'm a double agent for the humans," button on his jacket.

"Is it really an invisibility neutralizer?" the Chert salesman asked. "We were told that human technology was still in the semiconductor age."

"It worked pretty well just now," Lynx replied, giving the young man a friendly grin.

"Oh, you were joking. That's good," he said, displaying his bright yellow teeth in return. "Now that I think of it, if you had a working neutralizer, your temporary acting

194

junior consul wouldn't have been so surprised when I dropped by the embassy to reserve our folds. Can I interest you in our latest model? It's very stylish, popular with the up-and-coming professionals."

"I'm not sure I get the point of being stylish if nobody can see me," she pointed out. "So how does your invisibility technology work? I'm assuming it's that thing on your shoulder that keeps swiveling around like it's looking for something to shoot."

"We employ active photon replacement technology," the Chert rattled off the reply. "It tracks the eyes of biologicals and uses direct projection to overpower the reflected light you expect, substituting an image of the space behind the projector. It's an old trick, but we do it better than anybody else. If you wait until the end of the show, I could give you a deal on my display unit. That is, if you have anything interesting to barter."

"Let me take a look around the show and I'll get back to you," Lynx replied. "I wouldn't want to use up all of my ammunition here, only to find that the Vergallians are selling an astral projector that would let me be an invisible fly on the wall from the comfort of my home."

"Invisible fly on the wall," the young salesman repeated. "That's very good. I never heard it put that way before. Come back and see us any time. Or not," he concluded, vanishing along with the crowded booth in a blink of the eye.

Lynx fought the temptation to reach out and wave her hand through the space he had just occupied, to see if there was a body there or if she had been tricked by a hologram. Still, she had to admit that it was an effective sales pitch.

195

Sticking with the right side of the aisle so she wouldn't lose track of the booths she had visited, Lynx was immediately collared by a giant Dollnick, who gently gripped her shoulders with his lower set of arms and used the upper set to place a pair of well-padded headphones over her ears. There was a short burst of static, but then she heard herself saying, "I wouldn't want to use up all of my ammunition here, only to find that the Vergallians are selling an astral projector that would let me be an invisible fly on the wall from the comfort of my home."

The Dollnick took back the headphones, tossed them on the table, and held out his palm right in front of her nose. A small flying insect immediately came in for a landing, and Lynx had to blink several times before her eyes refocused at the short distance. It looked more like a micro-miniature bird than a fly, though it was so alien that it seemed silly to try to classify it. The Dollnick hadn't let go of her shoulders yet, so she sighed and tilted her head back, preparing to read him the riot act. Although they were big and acted confident, the Dollys always crumbled if you yelled at them.

"Why become a fly on the wall when you can have a fly do it for you?" the Dollnick asked, before Lynx could cut him down to size. "The Dollnick parrot-fly is the ideal proxy agent, and they are so cost effective that you can deploy them in swarms, covering all of the conversations at large events, like a trade show."

"Wait, you mean to tell me that this thing just listened in on my conversation with the Chert?" Lynx couldn't help being intrigued. "And it's not a little drone? It's a real bird-insect?"

"The parrot-fly is the result of hundreds of thousands of years of intensive breeding," the Dollnick launched into his scripted sales pitch. "It can operate independently in the field for up to a full cycle, as long as it has access to rotten fruit and water. The parrot-fly will automatically return to base when it nears its conversational storage capacity, leaving a trail of pheromones that will guide a replacement to the target. Parrot-flies are ecologically benign and approved for use on Stryx stations, and they can't be detected by the standard bug sniffers, which of course, are looking for electronic bugs. We're offering them at a special show discount of ten creds per thousand."

"Wow, that sounds incredibly cheap," Lynx replied honestly. "How do you get the parrot-fly to report the conversations it memorizes?"

"That requires a parrot-fly home base," the Dollnick explained smoothly, turning her towards the table where a gleaming hive-like structure about the size of a standard maintenance bot was displayed. "The home base allows you to move your swarm safely, includes a parrot-fly homing beacon, an emergency recall function, and of course, a full suite of audio amplification and transcription options."

"How much does the home base cost?" Lynx asked.

"The parrot-fly home base technology has been extensively field tested in battle conditions, and it is also used by the administrations of over three hundred star systems for search and rescue missions after natural disasters," the Dollnick continued, ignoring her question. "The home base requires no external power source. The hive employs a micro wind-turbine, powered by the beating wings of the parrot-flies in the dormitory section. If the local environment doesn't provide sufficient fruit and water, you can service the home base with an artificial mixture, which can sustain the full swarm for up to..."

"I can't afford it, can I?" Lynx interrupted him.

The Dollnick slumped. "Did you have to ask that?"

"Tough crowd today?" Lynx asked sympathetically.

"Damn Vergallians are selling parrot-fly pesticide in the next aisle," the Dollnick grumped. "My family has been breeding parrot-flies and parrot-dragon-flies for hundreds of generations, but this crowd all thinks they're old-fashioned. It's a good thing we've been building up the civilian side of the business."

"Parrot-dragon-flies?" Lynx inquired.

"Of course, to counter the parrot-flies," the Dollnick explained. "Most customers only buy one or the other. We never quite managed to train the dragons to recognize friendly parrots."

"I think I'll just take a look at what your nest-fellow is offering," Lynx said, disengaging from the disappointed parrot-fly salesman. She moved to the next Dollnick table, where the demonstrator was using three of his hands to display the spy-tech features of the watch he wore on his fourth wrist.

"Pull out on the winding stalk, and pow!" the Dolly exclaimed, carefully holding the tiny knob away from his other arms. "Invisible molecular filament, cuts through anything without active shielding."

"How do you get it back in again without accidentally lopping off a limb?" asked a Horten.

"The whole faceplate rotates like a reel and you wind it in," the Dollnick replied, using the forefinger from his third hand to spin the faceplate in rapid circles as he kept the molecular filament taut with his second hand's grip on the detachable stalk.

"What if you only have two hands?" Lynx asked.

"The watch also includes a superconducting magnet for manipulating or attracting ferrous objects," the Dollnick continued his pitch as if he hadn't heard her. "I won't demonstrate that here due to the number of you carrying Gem Nanotrackers today, but I assure you, it's a nifty technology for opening wooden doors with deadbolts on the opposite side."

"What's a deadbolt?" asked a Drazen.

"Who wears watches anyway?" the Horten chipped in. "And who builds wooden doors?"

"Did you get this out of an old James Bond movie?" Lynx asked. "I didn't realize anybody other than EarthCent agents watched them."

"I'm a double agent for EarthCent," the Horten declared proudly. He pointed at the button on his belt, which Lynx recognized but couldn't read, since the message was displayed in Horten and her translation implant only worked on speech.

"If you aren't buyers, just move along," the towering Dollnick said sulkily. He had already spotted fresh prospects over their heads and moved to intercept.

"Where's your button?" the Horten asked Lynx after looking her up and down.

"I actually am an EarthCent agent," she told him. "They didn't give me a button."

Eighteen

In accordance with their arrangement, Lynx and
Thomas met up with Blythe and Clive back at the
EarthCent booth at the end of the first day of the show.
Outside of the Nebulae room in the overflow area rented
to the Gem, they stopped in front of the large mapping
display for Nanotracker. Lynx readily spotted the avatar
that represented her and brought up the detailed tracking
information.

"Somebody's been drinking at lunch," Thomas
remarked, scanning down the verbose readout.

"It was just one beer, and it wasn't AT lunch, it was
FOR lunch," Lynx protested. "I'm starving now."

"You went by all sixty vendors?" Blythe asked in
surprise. "Did you actually talk to anybody, or did you
just run through stuffing free samples in your bag?"

Lynx looked down in embarrassment at the "EarthCent
Spy" bag most attendees toted about for free samples.
Hers was bulging so much that the handles didn't quite
touch when she gripped them in her hand.

"I skipped all of the bio-tech booths," she admitted. "I
don't want to start replacing my body parts that still work
fine."

"Still, it's good to know what we're up against," Clive
observed. "If we ever do have run-ins with alien agents,

remember that they may be more machine than man under the skin."

"Are you implying that there's something wrong with that?" Thomas asked pointedly.

"Oh look, it does transcripts," Blythe declared, zooming to the next level of detail for the Nanotracker. "As much as I hate to admit it, the Gem sure know how to spy."

"They get plenty of practice spying on themselves," Herl remarked, materializing out of thin air next to the group of humans. "And the problem with Gem tech is you never know if they're cloning the results, so you may effectively be sharing your intelligence with them. But they are good with the nanobots, I'll give them that."

"Did you just get here, Herl?" Blythe asked the Drazen spymaster. "I didn't see you come in."

"Oh, I'm a sneaky fellow," he replied. "I stayed in the background and watched the two of you recruiting double agents for a while. I have to say, it was one of the most amusing surveillance jobs I've done in my career. Some of the top alien agents working out of the station gave you their contact information and took your buttons. I can't understand why nobody ever thought of trying this before."

"It was Blythe's idea," Clive told him. "She figures that some of them will think that we're dumb enough to believe that they really are double agents. Plus, they'll feed us all sorts of phony intelligence for centees."

"What are we going to do with phony intelligence?" Lynx asked.

"Analyze it," Blythe answered. "If you figure the false intelligence represents what they want us to believe and where they want us to look, we might be able to figure out what they're trying to hide and we'll have a good idea where it isn't. They'll probably include some real intelligence on the other species as well, to make the misinformation look legitimate. In any event, it will give our analysts something interesting to work with while they're waiting for our field agents to start producing."

"Fascinating," Herl said. "Whatever gave you such a good idea?"

"We do a lot of customer satisfaction surveys for InstaSitter because you can never let your guard down in business," Blythe explained. "Lots of parents lie through their teeth, telling us how much little Joey enjoys a mixed vegetable dish for dessert instead of ice cream, that sort of thing. We cross-check the suspicious results next time we babysit little Joey, and sure enough, the mixed vegetables turn out to be part of a misinformation campaign."

"Speaking of mixed vegetables, I only had a beer for lunch," Lynx reminded them. "I wouldn't have even had that if they weren't giving it out free at the Frunge booth."

"You drank the Frunge beer?" Herl asked, his jaw dropping open.

"It didn't taste that bad," Lynx replied defensively. "Why?"

"Nothing," Herl replied quickly, though he looked rather concerned. "Supper's my treat if you'll settle for the food court. My expense account isn't as flexible as you might think when it comes to entertainment. I'm afraid there have been abuses over the years by my predecessors, and Drazen bureaucrats have long memories."

"We were planning on discussing the technology we saw at the show while the impression is still fresh," Clive told him as they headed down the corridor as a group. "Are you sure you won't be bored?"

202

"Not a bit," Herl replied, still watching Lynx out of the corner of his eye as if he expected her to faint or explode. "Ambassador Bork was right about you humans. Great fun."

"Oh, look! They've opened another Panda Pagoda branch here," Blythe exclaimed as they entered the food court. "Any objections?"

"It's all the same to me," Thomas replied.

"If we steal their recipe for General Tso's Chicken, we'll have enough money to buy all the fun gadgets at the show," Lynx suggested. "I've been all over Stryx space, and Panda Pagoda is the most successful human business I've seen."

"Good aggressive thinking, but since Panda Pagoda is a human business, our job is to prevent other species from stealing the recipe," Blythe pointed out. "Besides, we're not in a position to do anything with a secret recipe. You'd need a chain of restaurants for that."

"I was kidding, sort-of," Lynx replied, scanning the menutab at the table for her favorite lo mein, putting in the order, and passing the device to Herl. "I'm all set."

"So what must-have technology from the show do you think we really need to buy?" Clive asked her.

"I thought about that a bit," she answered, hungrily watching Panda Pagoda's counter as if she expected her food to appear within seconds of being ordered. "Based on how things have gone with us so far, I think we should put your money into countermeasures. It's probably better if we don't start sending agents into the field until we can do it without every intelligence service in the galaxy knowing who they are and where they're going before they even leave the station."

"Very wise," Herl commented, after he made his choice and passed the menutab to Clive. He seemed surprised that anybody who would drink Frunge beer would have an intelligent opinion.

"How about you, Blythe?" Clive asked as he studied the menu.

"I'll have my usual," she answered.

"No, I meant, what do you want from the show?"

"Right. The Drazen bug sniffers were impressive, but I really liked the Vergallian full-spectrum active suppression system, though we could never tell Kelly who makes it or she won't have it in the office."

"Do you think they would sell you one without a back-door?" Herl inquired.

"Isn't that something we could figure out and disable?" Blythe asked.

"Not on your own," Herl answered, and offered an expanded explanation. "Your scientists have some very, er, interesting views on how the universe works, but your technology base has a long way to go to catch up. Leaping forward in knowledge is just a matter of education, but if you could send all of your top people back in time to your Stone Age, it would still take them many generations to achieve even a crude facsimile of your current technology. It's a question of tools, of bootstrapping. There's no magical way to skip generations of technology, even if you know the final shape of things."

"So what do you suggest?" Clive asked.

"If I was in your shoes, I would buy competing versions of detection technology, but stay away from the intelligent active jamming," Herl replied. "A Drazen sniffer will reliably detect all the bugs we know of, and as a double-check, you could run a Vergallian or Dollnick sniffer to make sure a rogue Drazen entity isn't listening in without permission."

"A rogue Drazen entity?" Lynx repeated, raising an eyebrow.

"I'm sure you know that all espionage is commercial in nature," Herl replied. "There are Drazen businesses and inter-species consortiums that are better financed and equipped than my agency, and there are plenty of Drazen chain restaurants as well," he added significantly, tapping on the menu tab.

"How about you, Thomas?" Clive inquired. "See any must-have equipment?"

"I'm sure you noticed that some of the industrial consortiums were selling enhancements for artificial people and robots as well as biologicals," Thomas replied. "I believe I could easily integrate an electromagnetic spectrum jammer without a controller, and by handling the frequencies myself, I could secure any room I'm in against most active bugging. I know what's needed, I'm just currently short the proper hardware for the job."

"Anything else?" Blythe inquired.

"Some of the hidden weapons systems were tempting," the artificial person admitted. "I liked the laser pointer with the high-energy setting, and I have room for a couple of high-voltage stunner implants in my middle fingers. And the memory weapons were very impressive."

"I must have missed those," Lynx admitted to her partner. "I guess I shouldn't have skipped past the bio-tech stuff so quickly. Were the memory weapons based on Farling drugs? Could we have used them to erase the last hour of memory from the Vergallian spy Beowulf caught at the camp?"

"Not that type of memory," Thomas explained. "You probably saw them and walked right past between the demonstrations. They were on one of the Verlock tables, a mix of edged weapons and drinking cups, three-dimensional metal art works, chain mesh belts, all those things."

"I don't remember," Lynx replied, drawing a laugh from the others at her unintentional joke.

"Everything displayed was made from Verlock memory metal. So a coffee urn can transform itself into a rapier at a touch, a goblet becomes a dagger, a plowshare becomes a mace-head."

"And you think that walking around with a coffee urn, a goblet or a plowshare would help agents go unnoticed on an undercover mission?" Lynx asked skeptically.

"Any of them would fit into the trading stock we were provided with on Earth," Thomas pointed out.

"That was a one-time thing," Lynx replied. "Clive won't be sending our agents on trading missions with junk that people are trying to clean out of their houses."

"And what does the Director think we should be buying?" Blythe asked her husband.

"The interstellar tracking technology," Clive answered. "The Effterii is the only qualitative advantage we hold over any of the species, and with the exception of the Stryx, there's no ship it couldn't keep up with or outrun. But there's also no way I'm aware of to track ships through jumps unless you plant a beacon onboard. The Verlocks were selling some quantum-coupled directional finders they make by scavenging the parts from Stryx ship controllers and registers. Expensive, but they're supposed to be next to impossible to detect, and in the right situation, priceless."

"How about renting out to cover the cost?" Lynx suggested. "You could offer to do tracking jobs for other species, make them put down a deposit to cover the cost of the location finder if we don't get it back, and charge a nice fee on top to go after the target and provide the actual coordinates."

"Sounds like a good way to get shot at," Thomas said. "Does the Effterii have a weapons system? Can I come?"

A waiter brought the food, and Herl made several elaborate hand passes over his Moo Goo Gai Pan as if he were performing a magical or religious rite. Apparently satisfied with the results, he separated his chopsticks and began to eat.

"What was that all about?" Lynx asked, never one to let the opportunity to pose a question slip by. "I've eaten with plenty of Drazens, but I've never seen that ritual."

"I always check fast food," Herl explained, displaying a distinctive ring with a blue crystal which he wore on his fourth finger. "If it contains any substances I've added to the filter, the crystal will glow. Compared to you humans, we Drazen can eat almost anything, but I've found that MSG gives me a headache."

"You wear a ring just for that?" Clive asked, amused by the idea.

"It also checks for poison, of course, in food and in the air," Herl replied, as he expertly wielded the chopsticks to lift a mouthful of Moo Goo Gai Pan.

"Sounds like the kind of basic technology we should really be providing to our own agents," Blythe commented. "I don't recall anybody displaying food and air testers at the show, though."

"They really aren't considered intelligence technology, or even high-tech," Herl explained. "This particular model

I bought some years ago at a luggage shop, though it's also common to see them sold at street fairs, anywhere there are lots of small food carts."

"You know, I think I've seen them," Lynx said, taking a break from shoveling down her lo mein. "I kind of wondered why I kept seeing vendors selling the same cheap-looking rings in Drazen markets on the colonies where I've traded. I thought they were for kids. How come I never see humans wearing them?"

"You'd have to talk the manufacturers into producing a human version, or it would take years just to teach it to react to the items you can't eat," Herl told her. "Besides, humans are picky cross-species eaters because you know everything can hurt you. Drazens tend to get careless because we assume we can eat anything. The same is true for drugs."

"Would it bore everybody if told Herl about that vacation Lynx and I took?" Thomas asked cautiously, watching Blythe and Clive for a cue. "Perhaps he could suggest a simple technology that could help us avoid such incidents in the future."

"We don't have any secrets from Drazen Intelligence," Clive replied, without making it clear whether this was by agreement or a simple acknowledgement of the facts. So Thomas proceeded to regale the table with a tale of how Lynx became comatose after accidentally absorbing the Farling drug, and how he passed twelve days by her side, mainly watching the old spy movies provided by their original EarthCent handler under the guise of educational materials. Lynx recognized a number of embellishments, but given that the artificial person's previous job included telling bedtime stories, Thomas was practicing admirable restraint.

"So the Farlings are up to their old tricks," Herl commented, "Started with an anonymous tip, I'll bet."

"Was that you?" Blythe asked. "Thank you for the warning. The Stryx analyzed samples of the Farling drugs recovered after Thomas dumped them, and they immediately put four of them on the forbidden list. Horrible mind control and mind-destroying stuff."

"No, I thought you understood," Herl replied. "The anonymous tip was from the Farlings themselves, it's part of their standard marketing campaign. I'll send over the details when I get back to the Drazen embassy."

Nineteen

"It's been a couple of months since our last meeting, so before I ask Ambassador McAllister to get us caught up on what her agency head is doing, do we have any urgent business that needs to be addressed?" The unelected president of EarthCent paused to watch the holographic representations of the six ambassadors for a response.

"Just to make sure I'm straight on this, we're giving up on the code names and the zoo animal filter?" asked Mother.

"That's right, Belinda," President Lin confirmed. "The six of you were probably the only ones who weren't sure of who was who at our meetings, since the alien intelligence agencies certainly weren't fooled. In fact, you may as well all go around once and introduce yourselves so you won't feel foolish if you happen to meet at a conference. Would you start?"

"Belinda White, Hearth Station Ambassador," Belinda complied willingly. "I never cared for the cloak-and-dagger nonsense, I'm just in it for the intelligence. I see you found the funds somewhere to pay the Stryx for a secure channel."

"I borrowed the money from our lost and found," President Lin replied. "Hopefully, nobody comes back looking for a Dreeb skin purse full of Stryx creds, or we could have a problem. My office manager thinks it may have been intended as a bribe from one of the visiting delegations, but they're going to be disappointed since we don't even know who purchased our good will. Stephen?"

"Stephen Beyer, Void Station Ambassador," the former bird of paradise code named Troll introduced himself. "I hope everybody used the bug sweepers that Intelligence sent us by special courier."

"Special courier?" the ex-python known as Tinkerbelle commented with a laugh. "Mine was delivered to our apartment by the InstaSitter who came to babysit the kids last week."

"You have to admire that kind of efficiency," President Lin said, shaking his head in despair over the contrast with EarthCent's diplomatic organization. "Would you introduce yourself to the others?"

"Svetlana Zerakova, Corner Station Ambassador. The sweepers worked great, but I had to ask Farth to send a maintenance bot to actually remove the listening devices without destroying my embassy offices. Fortunately, the Stryx don't see cleaning up the bugs after they've been detected as violating their principles."

"Same here," the other ambassadors all echoed.

"Not having station maintenance bots on Earth, we were forced to tear our offices apart," President Lin admitted. "On the bright side, they were badly in need of remodeling, and I doubt the other species will go to the expense of sneaking in new bugs now that they know we can detect them. Carlos?"

"Carlos Oshi, Middle Station Acting Ambassador," the former elephant with the odd code name of Pill Bottle introduced himself. "I'm looking forward to hearing some good news on progress."

"Raj?" the president prompted.

"Raj Tamil, Echo Station Ambassador. I'd like to suggest a staggered schedule for future meetings so I'm not always getting up in the middle of the night for them."

"Does everybody know Kelly?" President Lin asked.

There was a chorus of assents, an unnecessary comment about Kelly's auctioneering attempt, and a gratuitous remark about frightening a young Stryx into a coma, all of which Ambassador McAllister took to mean that no introduction was necessary.

"First, let me say that the Oxfords are doing a fantastic job, and they are targeting the end of the year to begin producing regular reports on our list of action items," Kelly said. "I'm officially returning from maternity leave next Monday, and Blythe has already requested that I give her or her senior staff a regular meeting slot each week to make sure that our diplomatic and intelligence efforts remain in sync."

"Any progress on the Farling drug threat?" Ambassador Beyer asked.

"That's one of the things I was going to talk about," Kelly replied. "Thanks to our partnership with Drazen Intelligence, I've been provided with a case study of the traditional Farling business model. It turns out that the Farlings create a whole suite of horrific drugs for every new biological that appears on the galactic stage, and then they tip off the homeworld government. Their goal is to sell inoculations and neutralizers. Prevention is a much bigger and safer market than selling dangerous mind-destroying drugs to criminals, which would just get the Stryx mad in any case. I asked Ambassador Bork, and it appears that all of the advanced species enforce harsh penalties for mind control that make it a crime for suicidal maniacs. He couldn't find a single incidence of such a case

212

in the Drazen legal system for as long as their current record system reaches back."

"So the Farlings aren't evil incarnate?" Belinda asked. "I've always heard that they are a bunch of amoral genetic manipulators who stay out of Stryx space because they know their experiments wouldn't be tolerated."

"That's all true enough, but everybody would have gotten together and wiped them out long ago if they were that much of a threat," Kelly replied. "Many species use their drugs for suspended animation rather than freezing themselves for extended space travel. The Farlings are just as willing to cure a disease as to create one, as long as the price is right. They just don't see the rest of us biologicals as human, or maybe I should say, beetle."

"How about this public attempt to recruit double agents from alien intelligence agencies I've heard so much about?" Raj asked. "The Gem ambassador here buttonholed me at a party and said that she would view any such attempt on Echo Station as an act of aggression."

"Without going into great detail, I'm told that the Gem response to the double agent program has been, uh, atypical," Kelly replied.

"A trio of Fillinducks came into my embassy looking for the cultural attaché in an attempt to sign up," Belinda added. "I told them we hadn't been assigned a spy handler yet but to check back in a few cycles."

"Recruitment of double agents has been going well, but I'm only supposed to supply details on a need-to-know basis," Kelly told them. "Does anybody have a need to know?"

"I'd rather not," President Lin replied. "Anything else?"

"I'm glad you brought up the cultural attaché situation, Belinda," Kelly continued. "Intelligence will be graduating the first class of agents this weekend, and we're having a picnic at, er, the training camp. Filling the attaché slots, at least temporarily, is one of the top priorities for the Oxfords. And the second class is already well underway, as is recruiting for the third. So if you have any personal recommendations for agent trainees, please pass the names along when your cultural attaché arrives."

"How about your spy show?" the president asked. "That was officially an EarthCent event, correct?"

"Before we hear about that, I have a confession to make," Raj interrupted. "I was able to attend the first day of the show, and I seem to have overdone it at a party."

"You should have told me you were on the station, even though I was on leave," Kelly protested. "Or at least you could have stopped in at the embassy."

"I was worried about security, and I wanted to experience the show as a paying attendee," Raj explained. "As I was saying, I drank a bit too much and I might have been a little indiscreet with a certain young lady."

"Indiscreet?" Svetlana asked coldly. "What does that entail, exactly?"

"I'm not quite sure," Raj replied guiltily. "Nothing like this has happened before in my career. A woman asked me to buy her a drink, we started dancing, and the next thing I knew, a waitress was waking me up and asking if I wanted another bottle. I seem to remember discussing some things related to our committee work," he concluded in a deflated tone.

"Did the woman have a name?" Kelly asked.

"Just something she made up for the evening," Raj replied. "Who would name a daughter Chance?"

"I don't think you have anything to worry about," Kelly told him. "Chance is an agent, and I'm told she's the top of

214

the class when it comes to extracting information in bars. But it's a good learning opportunity for all of us, and it supports Clive's view that this committee focus on policy rather than getting involved in operational details."

"I've been reading through some of the so-called training materials that were provided to our original two agents, and I learned that the old national intelligence agencies usually had a cabinet minister or government appointee providing direct oversight and liaison to the government," the Void Station ambassador said. "It seems to me that Ambassador McAllister is already filling that role, and the whole operation is being run out of Union Station, so perhaps we should formalize her position."

"Excellent idea, Stephen," President Lin seconded the motion before Kelly could protest. "All in favor of appointing Ambassador McAllister the Minister of Intelligence, raise your hands. One, two, three, four, five, and myself. Excellent."

"How can I be an ambassador AND the Minister of Intelligence?" Kelly protested. "Besides, EarthCent isn't really a government, and even if it was, we're hardly a parliamentary system!"

"You're outvoted six to one," the president replied. "My staff will be thrilled that arranging and paying for these committee meetings is off our plate. Shall we call it a day?"

"What does being Minister of Intelligence have to do with running the committee?"

"Makes sense to me," Raj observed. "Please don't forget my scheduling request."

Kelly glared around the virtual table at her five fellow ambassadors and the EarthCent president, but they were all looking at somebody else when she tried to catch their eyes. "Fine," she growled. "Meeting adjourned."

The five holographic ambassadors winked out, but the president remained, holding up a finger to indicate he wanted a minute to talk alone.

"Yes, President Lin," Kelly said, stressing the title which carried little actual power in the distributed EarthCent hierarchy that had been imposed by the Stryx in any case.

"Just two things, Kelly," the president said mildly. "First, I want to thank you for expediting the return of my wife's family silver. I never would have heard the end of it."

"You're welcome," Kelly replied cautiously. "It's lucky our agent was in a coma for nearly two weeks so she didn't have time to sell it."

"Second, I just wanted to tell you, well, warn you really, that you showed up in the top five on the latest version of our depth chart."

"What depth chart is that?" Kelly asked before the meaning caught up with her. "No! You don't mean that if something happens to you, I'm in line to be the unelected president!"

"We're still officially wards of the Stryx," the president reminded her. "I don't know if we're one generation or a hundred generations away from being deemed responsible enough to self-organize, though I believe this intelligence agency is a step in the right direction. In the meantime, EarthCent depends on the Stryx for recruiting personnel, and even though we make our own decisions, I wouldn't claim for a minute that we are acting in accordance with the majority view of the humans we represent. Yet, it does seem to be working."

"So you're saying the Stryx have moved me into the number five slot?" Kelly asked, crossing her fingers.

"No, I'm saying you appear in the top five, but as you've become fond of saying lately, the exact slot is on a need-to-know basis," President Lin answered playfully. "Until the next meeting, then."

"Wait!" Kelly said to the empty space above her display desk. "I'm not even officially back from maternity leave yet," she concluded with a groan.

"Were you talking to me?" Libby asked.

"Libby!" Kelly cried, like a drowning woman grasping at the oar of the war galley that had just sunk her fishing boat. "No matter what, don't let them make me president. Promise!"

"It's not that simple," Libby replied after a pause. "I can only promise that you'll never become president against your will."

"Done!" Kelly declared, experiencing a wave of relief. "It's not just the job, you know. Union Station is our home now. I wouldn't know how to live somewhere without a ceiling, not to mention having to deal with the weather and all of those mosquitoes."

"At least you don't have parrot-flies on Earth," Libby remarked slyly. Parrot-flies? The office door was closed, but one of the Dollnick bio-bugs could have easily followed her all the way from Mac's Bones, going through the lift and the doors with her. Where was a Dollnick dragonfly when you needed one?

A line of illuminated dots appeared on the front display wall of her office, lighting up in sequence to point at a spot near the top of the door. Kelly removed her sandal and approached stealthily, pretending to be examining the stitching of the sole. When she was just beyond the detection range that triggered the door to open, she sprang forward, swinging the sandal at the spot indicated by the lights.

SPLAT! A small green stain appeared on the wall, matching a little pulped mass on the bottom of her sandal.

"As long as we're bending the noninterference rules today, how about an opinion on President Lin's assessment of our progress?" Kelly asked, as she reached in her purse for a bit of tissue to clean up the bug. Fortunately, she had a whole package of baby wipes, which made quick work of the remains.

"I'm not sure what you mean about bending the rules," Libby replied innocently. "On the subject of self-determination, you know that our policy is to protect humans from themselves. Have you seen the Grenouthian documentary about human democracy through the ages?"

"Aisha mentioned something about it, but I decided to pass when I saw it was listed as a comedy," Kelly admitted. "What's wrong with government by the people for the people?"

"It's a wonderful thing, and humans have occasionally achieved it in small groups where everybody knew each other. When we opened Earth, the elder Stryx determined that your electoral systems for selling offices were in large part responsible for the economic collapse that forced us to intervene. EarthCent, to the extent that it governs, is truly a government by the people for the people."

"But the Stryx pick the people," Kelly protested.

"Yes, and I believe we do a fine job, thank you very much," Libby responded dryly. "Back on Earth, your old national governments are nominally in charge, but all of the real work is done on the local level, providing basic services in return for fees. Integration into the galactic economy has provided all humans with the option to pick up and go elsewhere, to vote with their feet. EarthCent is the only official representative of humanity as a whole, and you don't see a line of people outside of the embassy every morning begging for more laws."

"But that's because the Stryx run everything on the station," Kelly protested again.

"That's not really true if you think about it," Libby replied. "We enforce a few laws related to property and interactions among species, but on the whole, station inhabitants are self-governing. Humans do very well as guests, and humans are guests everywhere but on Earth and a couple of modest colonies, which have so far avoided the governance problem through low population density."

"You're saying that people can only manage democracy if you split the 'demo' from the 'cracy'?" Kelly ventured, wondering if she had the Greek etymology correct.

"You really should watch the Grenouthian documentary," Libby answered. "Your electoral systems have always favored candidates who say what the people want to hear, and your great vice as a species is your ability to believe them. It's the same mechanism of believing in impossibilities, even when the outcome means life or death, that doomed your global economy."

"Well, all's well that ends well," Kelly said defensively. "If you hadn't bailed us out, I understand we would have been taken over by the Vergallians sooner or later."

Samuel woke up from his nap and made a "guh" sound.

"Did you hear that, Libby?" Kelly exclaimed, racing to pluck her nearly six-month-old out of his bassinet. "He said 'Ma!'"

"Didn't we just talk about humans hearing what they want to believe?" Libby inquired.

"Actually, I think you said we believe what we want to hear," Kelly retorted, setting Samuel down on the surface of her display desk. "Did you see that? He lifted his head and his chest. I think he's almost ready to crawl."

"So you put him on your desk near the edge?"

"Guh," Samuel repeated.

"He's trying to say 'Ma' again!" Kelly proclaimed proudly.

"It sounds more like he's trying to say 'Gryph,'" Libby observed.

"Up!" Kelly declared, lifting Samuel and heading for the door. "Mommy is taking baby home where the people aren't mean to us."

Twenty

The graduation ceremony for the first class of EarthCent Intelligence agents was held on the training grounds at Mac's Bones, followed by the typical McAllister picnic. Eighteen humans had completed the course, helping to create the curriculum for the next batch of trainees as they went along. Six of the graduates who showed diplomatic skills and were willing to move had been assigned to the cultural attaché program and would be shipping out to other Stryx Stations in the coming days. The remainder had been divided evenly into field agents and analysts, with the field agents to undergo further training as itinerant traders under Lynx's tutelage.

"This is the first spy school graduation I've ever attended," Bork told Kelly, as they stood together at the back of the line for the barbeque. "I'm not sure if that's because none of my friends ever became spies, or because Drazen Intelligence keeps the ceremonies secret."

"One of the things Clive insists on while he's running the agency is that we don't try to fool ourselves," Kelly explained. "He says that even with all the technology we picked up at the spy show and Drazen help in implementing it, we're a long way from being able to run a secret agency. For the time being, he thinks we're better off just operating in the open and learning what works as we go along."

"What were the little packages Blythe was handing out to the graduates?" Bork asked.

"That's on a need-to-know basis," Kelly told the Drazen ambassador sternly, then dissolved in laughter when he appeared to take her seriously. "They each received a programmable Stryx cred linked to the InstaSitter register, it's how Blythe handles payroll. I wish the embassies used the same system, it would save a lot of aggravation."

"And where are your offspring today?" Bork inquired, noticing that Kelly wasn't carrying Samuel, and Dorothy wasn't running circles around them.

"Donna babysat for them inside during the ceremony," Kelly replied. "She's probably playing a game with Dorothy since they aren't out yet. Blythe was annoyed that I didn't call for an InstaSitter, but Donna is trying to send her a message."

"What message is that?" Blythe asked, joining the line behind them. "Clive, did my mother say anything to you?"

"Just the usual," Clive replied, ostentatiously counting the people between them and the grill. "Did you get a chance to talk to Kelly about the Gem double agents? Maternity leave is over tomorrow, right?"

"Actually, the six months was officially up at 02:37 this morning, but I don't go into the office weekends unless there's something important," Kelly admitted. "You did tell me about the strong double agent response during the show, and I heard through channels that some of the other embassies are getting grief from the local Gem ambassadors, but I just assumed that the clones are suffering from groupthink. They all have the same brain, after all."

"The Gem appear to be the only species whose agents took our offer literally," Clive explained. He paused to remove a Drazen sweeper from his tunic and checked for bugs as the line shuffled forward. "All of the other double agents volunteered in order to feed us false information."

"And to get the cool button," Blythe added in an I-told-you-so undertone.

"But the Gem double agents are actually hoping to work against their own government," Clive continued. "Apparently, there's a growing clandestine movement to reestablish the original genetic lines of the species from samples kept on file by the Farlings. I passed the information along to Herl, of course, but it's more of a diplomatic issue than an intelligence issue as far as we're concerned."

"Herl did mention it, and we've been bringing it up quietly with the other species," Bork responded after checking his own bug detection device. Then he took a little box from his pocket and released a dragonfly. "The station is infested. Better safe than sorry."

Over at the traditional McAllister table, Lynx asked Tinka, "So you're going to keep working for InstaSitter even while you serve as our liaison to Drazen Intelligence?" She batted with the back of her hand at a parrot-fly attacking her fruit salad and missed. "Aren't you kind of young to be spreading yourself so thin?"

"Your headquarters and analysts are going to be sharing our office space, and I doubt it will take more than a few minutes of my time," Tinka replied causally. "It makes sense because both sides trust me, but I'm sure Clive and Blythe will work directly with Herl for anything really important. I'll be more of a Drazen filter for your analysts than anything else."

"You owe me eighty creds," Jeeves announced, appearing out of nowhere. The Stryx dropped a flat plastic

223

box in front of Lynx, coincidentally crushing the parrot-fly. A disappointed dragonfly veered off and began hunting for fresh prey. "If you're going to keep up with this hobby, you should talk to Kelly about sneaking your film into the diplomatic pouch. It will take even longer to get back that way, and from what you told me, waiting is half the fun."

"What is it?" Tinka asked out of curiosity, never having seen a similar package.

"My prints are here!" Lynx exclaimed, pushing aside her plate and opening the box. "Look how sharp they are, and it's the first time I used that camera!"

"Vacation images on paper?" Tinka asked, looking curiously at the collage of photographs that spilled out on the table. "And who's the cute guy with the yellow eyes?"

"That's a picture of the Chert who was selling invisibility projectors at the trade show," Lynx replied, looking at the off-center image of the slightly-out-of-focus alien. "But I took this picture when I couldn't see him. I thought I was joking when I claimed the camera was an invisibility field neutralizer."

"Highly effective," Jeeves commented. "Just take an exposure with chemical-based film that the invisibility projector doesn't recognize as an optical detection system, send it back to Earth by the fastest means available, and in approximately ten days, you'll know if there was somebody standing in front of you swinging an axe."

"I don't believe it!" Tinka exclaimed, holding up another photograph in front of her face as if she were about to kiss it. "You have a picture of Jeelop Huir! He's so gorgeous and—Ick! You photographed him going to the bathroom?"

"Let me see that." Lynx grabbed at the print, not knowing who Tinka was talking about. "Oh, yeah. That's the Horten guy on Seventy who almost caught us. I didn't see what he was doing until I took the picture because I was focusing on his face. Operating a camera isn't like just looking at something and saving it on your implant."

"But he's the biggest Horten immersive star! They say he gets thirty million cred per production." Tinka took the picture back from Lynx and stared at the image in puzzlement. "What would he be doing on a Farling world dressed like a Forest Knight. Do you have any other pictures?"

Lynx separated the Farling Seventy prints from the pictures of the spy show and the other odd shots she'd taken to use up the roll, and pushed them over to Tinka. The Drazen girl studied the prints, frowning and shaking her head. "There's something funny going on. That looks like an immersive production crew to me. Is Ambassador Bork here?"

"He's coming now," Lynx replied, as Kelly and Bork approached the table with heavily laden plates. "Over here, we saved you seats." Clive and Blythe followed just a few paces behind the ambassadors.

"Are those your show photos?" Clive asked. "Don't forget to submit the receipt for development."

"She has a picture of Jeelop Huir that she took on Farling Seventy," Tinka told Bork before the Drazen could even sample his hamburger. "Never mind what he's doing. Look at the uniform and these other pictures."

Bork accepted the prints in his fatherly way, as if to humor the young Drazen woman. But in a matter of seconds, his expression changed from amusement, to incredulity, to anger.

"They're doing the Battle of Scort Woods," the Drazen ambassador said hollowly, almost as if he'd received a

225

blow. He turned to Lynx and asked, "When were these taken?"

"Maybe a week after we left Earth, a little over four months ago," Lynx replied. "I could check with Thomas."

"Did I hear my name?" Thomas said, looking up from his conversation with Jeeves at the end of the table.

"Do you remember when we took these pictures on Seventy?" Lynx asked.

"Seems like yesterday," Thomas replied, and then thought for a bit. "No, it couldn't have been yesterday because we were here. It must have been a while ago."

"Call it four and a half months," Lynx told the Drazen ambassador, kicking herself for having asked the time-impaired artificial person for help with a date.

"The production would be finished by now," Bork said fiercely, his tentacle rising behind his head. Then he lapsed into silence, staring at the prints as he carried out a subvoced conversation with somebody, probably transmitting the images through his implant as well.

"What's this all about?" Kelly asked Lynx and Tinka.

"DHP, Drazen Historical Productions, are making the Battle of Scort Woods for the new season," Tinka explained. "Don't you get Galactic Entertainment Guide? DHP only produces one really big budget historical drama a season, and it looks like the Hortens are trying to jump our ratings."

"What was the Battle of Scort Woods?" Kelly asked.

"It took place hundreds of thousands of years ago, I once visited the planet to see the battlefield," Clive stepped in to explain. "It was soon after the Hortens joined the galactic community, and they and the Drazens were very active in one of the orders of knights that kept the peace on the fringes of Stryx space. Scort was a technology ban

226

world almost completely covered in forest, and the knights fought an epic battle against the Pullrip, who are fire breathers. The Pullrip never have joined the tunnel network, and their empire remains out-of-bounds today."

Bork came out of his trance looking even angrier than before. "Jeelop Huir is back on Horten Eight, but our people lost track of him for several months when he was supposedly taking a long honeymoon with his new wife. Herl has already contacted DHP to warn them and apologize for the intelligence breakdown. This is going to be very expensive for somebody."

"So we've scored our first intelligence coup," Kelly declared triumphantly. "But why are you so unhappy?"

"The Battle of Scort Woods was my vacation role," Bork explained, his tentacle drooping to half-mast in disappointment. "I went as a background actor, but the director bumped me up to a full knight position and gave me a speaking part. I've never had a line before."

"Maybe they'll just delay the release date a few cycles, give people a chance to forget the Horten version," Tinka suggested. She didn't look particularly disappointed, and Kelly got the impression she would rather see Jeelop Huir playing the lead role than Ambassador Bork delivering his first line.

"More like a thousand cycles, and that's assuming DHP doesn't cut their losses and abandon the project before they finish shooting the interior scenes," Bork grumbled. Then he stood up, placed one hand on his chest, held an imaginary sword over his head and proclaimed, "Let death be my bride today!"

Everybody clapped politely.

"Where's Chance?" Lynx asked Thomas. "She was on the orbital when the Hortens were shooting the immersive on Seventy and she might know something about it."

"She probably hid after the ceremony," Thomas replied. "Chance isn't really that comfortable in social situations with humans unless there's drinking and music. If you need to find her, just ask yourself, 'If I was an artificial person hiding in Mac's Bones, where would I be?'"

"You are an artificial person, Thomas," Kelly reminded him.

"Oh, right," Thomas responded cheerfully. "I guess she's over there behind the tug, then. I'll go check."

Lynx moved down next to Jeeves when Thomas rose. She wasn't yet comfortable talking with the disembodied voices of station Stryx, and she had some questions she was hoping to get answered.

"I suppose you'll want a receipt for the developing now," Jeeves remarked.

"Don't worry about it," Lynx told him. "When I originally took this job, I was supposed to pay myself and Thomas through trading profits, maintain my ship, and remit the surplus to the home office. Since Blythe and Clive took over, I get a salary that's more than I've earned in years, and any trading profits are mine to keep."

"My partners and I have talked it over, and our auction business will be subscribing to your intelligence feed when you get it up and running," Jeeves told her. "Some of my elders are skeptical that I can restrain myself from using information that would take unfair advantage of any competition, so I'm keeping myself on a very short leash when it comes to business intelligence."

After reflecting on the meaning of the Stryx's words, Lynx said, "That can't be much fun. You must see your

228

partners making mistakes and missing opportunities all of the time, and not be able to say anything about it."

"You and I are both outsiders in a way," Jeeves observed. "We Stryx don't have a government in any human sense of the word. We're all free agents, but free will loses a good deal of its meaning when everybody agrees on the path forward."

"Are you feeling alright, Jeeves?" Lynx inquired in concern. "I've heard that the original Stryx were designed around a set of stable solutions to the equations of self-awareness, but you sound a bit depressed."

"Would you invite me to a poker game?" Jeeves asked suddenly. "I promise not to keep track of which cards are which, or monitor any biological signs other than facial expressions."

"I'll play with you, Jeeves, but I don't know that any strangers would be willing," Lynx replied honestly. The Stryx's conversation was so strange that she began to wonder if he was trying to lead her somewhere, so she threw out a line to see if he would give it a yank. "I'm sure Paul and Joe would set up a game for you. Why are you asking me?"

"Because you're a genuine gambler," Jeeves replied, making it sound like she had solved a problem for him. "You started a new life based on a coin flip."

Lynx felt a tingle at the back of her neck that ran through her shoulders and down her arms, as if she had read a ghost story before bed and then had the feeling that somebody else was in the room. She bit back on a dozen immediate questions to put together the clues that Jeeves was feeding her, guessing that it might be a one-time opportunity.

"If the Stryx all agree on the necessary shape of the future, wouldn't you have to use your resources to keep it on the right path?" Lynx asked softly. "Does everybody in the galaxy have free will except for the puppet masters?"

"Free will is overrated," Jeeves practically snorted. "You've had free will your whole life, but you're still on the path to become the next head of EarthCent Intelligence."

"The guy who recruited me in the bar on Earth was a stringer hitting on redheads at random," Lynx replied in objection to the Stryx's implication.

"Do you think a low-rent theatrical agent would miss the chance to make an extra hundred creds by 'randomly' picking a person who had been described to him?" Jeeves asked.

"I flipped the coin too," Lynx insisted, after digesting the fact she had been chosen by the Stryx after all. "I could have walked away."

"You flipped a programmable Stryx cred," Jeeves corrected her. "Programmable."

"But that's just the amount!" she protested. Jeeves placed a programmable cred flat on the table, and Lynx watched in dismay as the amount and the image of the space station swapped back and forth. "Alright, so I waited ten years to be offered a job with EarthCent and I got it. It's just that I'm a spy rather than a diplomat."

"And I'm an auctioneer and a puppeteer," Jeeves replied.

"What are you two talking about down there?" Kelly called.

"Nothing," Jeeves and Lynx answered simultaneously.

Kelly gave them her best cynical look before returning to her self-appointed task of to trying to cheer up the

Drazen ambassador. A little bell went off in her head, and this time it was her mother calling.

"Are you busy now?" her mother inquired. "One of your nephews is talking about joining the next colony ship and I want you to stop him."

"I'm in the middle of a graduation picnic," Kelly subvoced back. She checked quickly to see if Bork was waiting for her to say something, but he and Clive had started a discussion about the aftermath of the Battle of Scort Woods. "Why do you want me to talk him out of it?"

"Because I've learned that when family members leave Earth and say they'll come back to visit as often as they can, it's all hot air," her mother pointed out mildly. "I don't suppose it occurred to you to use any of your maternity leave to bring my newest grandson to visit?"

"Babies hate Zero-G," Kelly replied, seizing on the first excuse she could think of. "Anyway, it's back to work for both of us tomorrow. You know that you and dad are welcome to visit us anytime."

"We didn't want to make extra work for you while you were involved with setting up the new spy agency," her mother replied. "Did the graduation go well?"

"It was supposed to be secret!" Kelly reacted in surprise "Maybe not secret-secret, but at least not common knowledge. How did you find out?"

"Dorothy keeps me up-to-date," her mother explained. "Such a smart little girl, she reminds me of your sister at that age. I'll let you get back to your picnic."

Kelly was still trying to get over the fact that she had a spy in her own household, when the little girl in question appeared at her shoulder. Dorothy put an index finger to her lips, and let her mother see a strangely familiar device that looked like a tiny flashlight in her other hand.

Donna finally arrived carrying Samuel, who had a small pair of goggles strapped over his eyes, reminding everybody of those cute "baby wearing sunglasses" advertisements. She placed him face down on the end of the table, and he immediately lifted his head and looked up and down the row of adults. Then he raised his chest, and began to squirm forward.

"He's crawling," Kelly cried in excitement and spread her arms out to welcome her six-month-old. "Come to Mommy, my precious."

Everybody along the table pulled their plates and drinks out of the way as Samuel picked up speed, but he went right past his mother and charged into Blythe's chest. Donna had worked her way around the table to behind Kelly by this point, and she whispered in the ambassador's ear, "We raided your free samples bag from the show." Then Kelly recognized the device in Dorothy's hand. It was the ultraviolet projector for the pathfinder goggles the baby wore.

Blythe stripped the goggles off of Samuel's little head and looked suspiciously into his baby blue eyes.

"It's the extra-purple light," Dorothy proudly whispered to her mother. "We trained Sammy to crawl to it."

Blythe picked up the baby and half grudgingly, settled him on her lap.

"Buh," Samuel declared in satisfaction.

EarthCent Ambassador Series:

About the Author

E. M. Foner lives in Northampton, MA with an imaginary German Shepherd who's been trained to bite bankers. The author welcomes reader comments at e_foner@yahoo.com.

Made in the USA
Las Vegas, NV
31 January 2021

16851055R00142